T0166748

PENGUIN

IF ONLY THEY KNEW

Anita Othman is a born and bred Malay Singaporean who grew up with a love of reading at a young age. Second-hand bookstores became her second home for many years. She graduated from the National University of Singapore with a degree in Literature and English Language. She was a civil servant for more than a decade until her husband was posted to Germany. As a result, she stopped working and joined him together with their daughter. With time on her hands, she focused on her love of creative writing. After Germany, the family moved to Jakarta where she became a regular columnist for the *Jakarta Globe* and *Jakarta Post*. On her return to Singapore, she started on her debut novel while pursuing a Diploma in Sports Science. Her novel *Still Waters* was published in 2021.

If Only They Knew

Anita Othman

PENGUIN BOOKS

An imprint of Penguin Random House

PENGUIN BOOKS

USA | Canada | UK | Ireland | Australia
New Zealand | India | South Africa | China | Southeast Asia

Penguin Books is part of the Penguin Random House group of companies
whose addresses can be found at global.penguinrandomhouse.com

Published by Penguin Random House SEA Pvt. Ltd
9, Changi South Street 3, Level 08-01,
Singapore 486361

First published in Penguin Books by Penguin Random House SEA 2023

ISBN 9789815058086

Typeset in Garamond by MAP Systems, Bangalore, India

www.penguin.sg

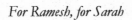

For Ramesh, for Sarah

Chapter 1

Singapore, 2010s

Saloma slid her car keys into her tailored trousers and made her way out of the multistorey car park, humming a tune under her breath. It was barely eleven in the morning, but the air was thick, making her sleeveless white blouse cling to her back. She crossed the heated black asphalt road and stepped onto the concrete pavement which led her to a towering cluster of public-housing apartments, in hues of red, blue, and yellow. Built in the 1970s, the apartments in Ang Mo Kio had since been given a facelift, with illuminated block numbers prominently displayed on the left and right side of each building, making it impossible to miss.

Wiping her nape, she was glad that she had persuaded her hairdresser to cut her hair short, after always having worn it long. Fishing for her oversized sunglasses from her tote bag, she perched them on her straight nose, relieved that they obscured her face and shielded her from prying eyes. She quickened her steps until she reached the newly constructed covered linkways that connected the residential apartment blocks to the basic amenities in the neighbourhood, glad for the shade they provided. Her low-heeled pumps clacked on the cement floor, startling a stray cat that was licking its paws. Saloma laughed and shooed it away as it glared at her from a distance.

She faltered when she spied a man rummaging through the rubbish bins, picking out cardboard boxes, and placing them in his rusty shopping cart which still bore the name of a famous supermarket. He looked up when he heard her. His face was scored by wrinkles, and his shrunken body looked almost child-like.

Saloma lifted her hand in acknowledgement but didn't wait to see his response. He was a familiar figure in the estate, often seen digging through piles of rubbish and dumpsters for cardboard boxes. He hauled them to a recycling centre when he had collected a sizeable amount of twenty to thirty kilograms for a meagre two dollars. When asked, he explained that he wanted to keep himself busy, to get his body moving, but many knew that it was his only source of income.

Saloma stepped onto the familiar ground floor of her mother's apartment block. It was airy and wide, meant for the residents to gather and meet. A curved stone table, shaped like a crescent moon, was right at the centre—a popular spot for housewives to chat in the day and lovers to meet at night. Several bicycle racks lined one wall.

It's funny Saloma mused, that it was only through a game of Pictionary Singapore Edition that she realized that the name Ang Mo Kio was in reference to Johnson Turnbull Thomson, a Government Surveyor of the Straits Settlement from 1841–53 who had built a bridge over the Kallang River. She had burst out laughing when it was made clear that the name Ang Mo Kio was taken from Hokkien and meant 'red-haired man's bridge,' where *ang mo* was a term for a Caucasian.

However, her English friend Greg was not too pleased with it and caused an awkward pause in the friendly game.

'I've never cared for that term. It's really not nice to be referred to as red-haired,' he said to the stunned locals seated at the table.

'But several of my Caucasian colleagues, even my boss, described themselves as such,' spluttered May. 'I don't think it's a derogatory term!'

'Any label given to a race is unacceptable,' Greg had retorted. 'Surely, none of you like the labels attached to your race.' He had looked at Saloma, 'You're called a *minah*, someone who is uneducated and you Steph, an *ah lian* for being a female Chinese version and Jack, you're an *ah beng*, the stereotypical male version.'

Saloma had watched the proceedings with amusement and had found the evening a refreshing change from the usual polite exchanges she was used to.

'Wah, Saloma is that you?' a voice called out.

Saloma turned to the direction of the voice and saw three men, probably in their seventies, hunched over a round table. They were perched on stools in the shape of tree stumps. One of them waved at her, his face alight with laughter, revealing a gold front tooth.

'Come and join us! So long we haven't seen you!'

'Hi, Uncle Edward. Yes, I've been busy,' Saloma answered, taking off her sunglasses and sliding them on top of her head. Up close, she saw that they were playing chess, on the stone-table chessboard.

'Wah, you're prettier and prettier! Can be a model.'

'*Swee*!' One of them spoke out in Hokkien, pushing his glasses back up so that he could see her better.

'Um . . . thanks. Carry on with your game, I don't wish to disturb you,' Saloma said, moving towards the lift lobby.

'*Aiyah*, how can you disturb us! We're retirees, nothing to do! We sit here all the time, looking at each other. Right or not,' he asked, looking at his two friends.

They nodded dutifully.

'Come, come sit with us. You can take my seat! Tell us about your life. Your mother said that you meet many important people.'

'Mother?' the man with the glasses asked.

'Aiyah, pay attention! She's Madam Marina's daughter!'

'Madam Marina?'

'Forgive this blur Uncle, Saloma. He's from the next block, so he knows nothing. Marina is my next-door neighbour,' he said, turning to the man with the glasses. 'She's the one who sold us *epok-epok* last week, and sometimes, she sells *nasi padang* dishes too.'

Saloma winced.

'Ah, that's your mother? She makes very good *kueh*. Can you cook like her?' the man with the glasses asked.

'Aiyah, don't ask stupid questions! Of course, she can cook! Her mother told me so but, not Malay kueh right?' Uncle Edward asked.

'Um, what do you mean?' Saloma asked.

'Your mother said that you only make ang mo food. I'm trying to remember,' Uncle Edward said, looking past her. 'Italian or French food, I think, but I forgot the name.'

'I do?' Saloma replied and inched her way to the lift.

'Forget about the lift. It's under repair. You can see the sign from here,' Uncle Edward said, pointing to the lift.

'Oh, really. It'll be a good exercise for me then,' Saloma said with a smile and walked away.

'I heard Marina said that Saloma is going to live in a big apartment. Penthouse, I think. Very rich. Strange that Marina is selling food. She doesn't get money from her daughter, *meh*?' Saloma overheard one of the men talking.

'Shhh . . . mind your business,' Saloma heard Uncle Edward shushing him.

Saloma slipped on her shades and stopped in front of the elevator. True enough, a big sign was posted on the decorated glass windows of the twin green doors. She'd always wondered about the design of the glass windows and the person who came up with it. They appeared so random: vertical dog bones, fish tails, diamond-shaped and S-shaped patterns. Tucking her hair behind her ear, Saloma looked up at the flight of stairs and was grateful that she only had to walk up four flights.

* * *

'Mummy?' Saloma called out, alarmed that the metal gate and the wooden front door were wide open.

She took off her shoes and stepped inside the modest three-bedroom apartment, her footsteps silent on the vinyl plank flooring. The smell of fried salted fish was heavy in the air.

A three-seater fabric sofa pushed against the wall and a beaten-up leather armchair faced the television. The vinyl record player she got for mother's last birthday was on the coffee table, and the P. Ramlee and Saloma vinyl records were next to it. Saloma smiled. It was quite a feat, sourcing a good recording of something that was made in the 50's and 60's.

The plain white walls were empty except for a framed black-and-white photograph of her parents. Her father wore a brown suit and her mother, a tight fitted *kebaya*, the tiny gap between her two front teeth obvious in her wide smile.

'Mummy?' she called out. 'Are you in the bathroom?'

She pushed the aluminium bathroom door wide open, but it was empty.

'Sal? Is that you?' her mother asked, walking out of her bedroom.

'Mummy, there you are! Why are your metal gate and front door wide open? Your padlock is just hanging loosely on one of the grilles. Anybody could just walk in and rob you!' Saloma exclaimed, as she watched her petite mother dry her hair with a towel.

'What is there to rob?' her mother asked, running her fingers through her damp hair. 'This?' she asked, pointing to the leather armchair. 'Or maybe this television? But then, it's old model. See, nothing to rob.'

'Mummy, it's still not safe. You live here all alone. Anyone can just walk in and attack you,' Saloma insisted.

'Attack? At my age? What do they say?' she asked, cocking her head to one side.

'I am no spring chicken,' she said, with a burst of laughter. 'And I not afraid to die,' she continued.

Saloma swallowed a sigh.

'So why did you leave the door wide open?'

'I fried salted fish last night. The smell of fish still there this morning. So, I open all windows doors. No need to stress. I don't hear you come in because hair dryer too loud,' her mother explained. 'Eh, what happen to you?'

'What?' Saloma asked, looking at herself.

'You *so* dark!' her mother said, peering closer. 'Go beach? Swim?'

Saloma heaved a sigh. 'Mummy, have you been outside? It's about 30–34 degrees Celsius and with the humidity, it's so much higher. What do you expect me to wear?' Saloma asked, irritated. 'Long sleeves, hat, gloves, trousers and . . . and an umbrella when I go out? And yes, my skin does get tanned so easily. I can't change that!'

'Eh . . . eh! Why so angry? I only asking. Why you here? Three months you don't come,' her mother asked, making herself comfortable on the leather armchair.

'To see you!' Saloma replied with a sigh, taking a seat on the sofa. 'And it's good to see you,' Saloma insisted.

'Hmm . . . you always come two times a month, but not now. Why?'

'I've been busy, I told you. But I call you every week,' Saloma countered. 'Have you worn the loungewear I got you?'

'Huh? Loungewear?'

'It's clothes to wear at home; it's the set I got you,' Saloma said to her mother's puzzled face. 'It's the floral-patterned blouse and the matching brown drawstring trousers,' she expanded.

'Oh, that one. Still in cupboard. I like what I wear. More comfortable.'

Saloma looked at the frayed blue cotton top and batik sarong that had undergone many washings. She bit her lip.

'Not good enough for you?' her mother asked, as she shifted in her seat. 'I'm always at home. My friends got no problem when they see me. Only you. Maybe, I change clothes when I go to your house. But I dunno when I get invitation,' her mother said, with a sidelong glance at Saloma.

'Mummy, you're welcome to my house any time. Why do you keep saying that? It's you who doesn't wish to come to my place!'

'Eh, how clever you blame me,' her mother sniffed.

Saloma stared at her mother's stiff profile and the straight line of her mouth. 'Did you have your hair done?' she asked, changing the subject. 'It looks shorter. And did you colour it too?' Saloma asked, reaching out to touch the top of her mother's head which had a purplish hue.

'Yes, is it nice?' her mother asked, turning her head from left to right. 'You know Cindy, my neighbour,' to which Saloma shook her head. 'You always forget,' her mother said with a scowl. 'She said a hairdresser just moved in upstairs, On the tenth floor. My *uban*, got too much. I went upstairs and she so nice. We both speak broken English. We laughed and laughed. She cut my hair, cover white hair, and make a little purple colour on top. "For fun" she said. She also said not to worry as it go away after many washings. I met Aunty Cindy's granddaughter at the lift and said that I look, what she said?' her mother stopped, closing her eyes. 'Ah, she said I look cool!'

'Why didn't you call me? I would have driven you to my hairdresser. I would have also arranged a manicure for you at the same time!'

'And make you shy? Or you make me change clothes? I don't need all that. And why must I pay for people to . . . to *manicure*, is it to cut nails?'

Saloma nodded.

'I can do myself! I have good nail cutters!'

'Mummy . . . you know, I didn't mean that. I just want you to have a little pampering. And what do you mean that you'll embarrass me?'

Her mother reached for a newspaper on the coffee table and started fanning herself.

Saloma closed her eyes for a moment.

'Isn't the fan working?' Saloma asked, looking up at the ceiling.

'Of course. I just want to save electricity.'

'Isn't the money I've given you enough? You should have told me. I could easily top it up!'

'Sal, you panic. Again. I don't need more of your money. I have enough, *cukup*, by selling my kueh and my nasi padang dishes.'

'I don't understand why you have to do this! It's ridiculous! I can perfectly support you and even move you to a better flat, a bigger flat.'

'What for? This is my home. You grow up here. You forget so fast. For me, this is enough. And I like cooking. I make money from it. Nothing wrong. Only you embarrass. For you, to give me money is a way to tell your friends you save your poor weak mother.'

'Mummy, you're hardly old or weak! Everyone has said that you don't look your age. And Aunty Samantha said something about you getting a couple of marriage proposals?'

'Humph! That Samantha speak rubbish. And why would I marry again? Your father is the only one.'

'Yup, and how did he repay you, Ma?'

'Eh, now you call me Ma? Always been Mummy. Mummy this, Mummy that.'

'But who taught me that! It was Daddy who said that the only way out of poverty, was through education and good social skills. Throughout my childhood, he stressed the importance of good manners and proper etiquette. Wasn't he the one who said that if there is a 100 metre race, people like us begin at the start line, but the Chinese are already at the 50 metre mark just based on their birth right.'

'Wah, so easy to blame him when he no longer here. Shame on you.'

Saloma looked at her seventy-year-old mother and wondered why she even bothered.

'Have you eaten?' her mother asked.

'Huh. What? Are we talking about food now?'

'I know you don't like my fried fish, but I have rice and eggs. I can fry egg with *kicap*. It was your father's favourite. He always asked for it when he came home late from work.'

'No thanks, Mummy. I'm not hungry. And have you ever wondered why he came home late? He was a civil servant, after all. Didn't they end work at five?' Saloma insisted.

'I never ask. Important is that he come home to me every night.'

'Okay, Mummy, whatever,' Saloma said, as she stood up and shrugged her tote bag further up her shoulder.

'You're leaving?'

'Yes, I'm meeting Su-Ann and Janice for lunch.'

'You contact them still? They went to school with you, right?'

'Yes, we lost touch after I got married but somehow, through social media, we got connected again.'

'Hmm.'

'Why, why do you ask?'

'Nothing. Just that they not your type.'

'Type, what type are you talking about?'

'Just that. Su-Ann is a teacher and Janice a housewife?'

'Su-Ann is still teaching, though I think she may quit, and Janice used to work but she gave it up when she had her children. They're my oldest friends and I care for them. Of course, they don't move in the same circles as I do but that's understandable cos Noah and I must entertain. He has his business and I have mine. My jewellery business, remember?' Saloma stressed, seeing her mother's puzzled look.

'Oh, you still have that business. I thought you close it down?'

'Mummy, sometimes, I think you're not listening when I share my life with you. It was challenging at one point, but I didn't give up. In fact, it's doing well, and a few magazines want to interview me about my success. They seem to think that I'm an inspiration to other woman,' Saloma said, her cheeks red.

'You must be happy. You always like people to praise you. How's your Noah?' her mother asked, changing the subject.

'He's good. Busy with work.'

'You still use his name?'

'What? You mean my married name?' to which her mother nodded.

'I don't understand, why you change your name to his. I didn't change mine when I got married.'

'Mummy, he's my husband. It's a natural thing to do. All my friends took their husband's name when they got married.'

'Yes, your *western* friends, your ang mo friends.'

Saloma winced.

'We in Singapore don't,' her mother continued. 'We keep our name till we die. But you are *Mrs* Salem.'

'Mummy, for someone who still pines for her dead husband of fifteen years, I thought you of all people will understand this!'

'Rubbish. Nothing to do with marriage, Sal. Taking his name make you important.'

'That's not true! We were both civil servants when we got married. We lived a regular life. Met regular people.'

'Yes, but his parents rich people. And then when they died, he became rich. You and him stop teaching and open tuition centres. I heard he got many centres now.'

'What's wrong in wanting to be our own bosses? And it just seemed easier if we both have the same name. That's all. This is getting absurd and silly. I must go. I'll see you next week.'

'Don't come then. I always alone.'

'Mummy, please don't start this. I'll come by next week,' Saloma said, bending down to kiss her on her cheek as they both walked to the front door.

'Be careful. Why need a fast car when traffic lights are everywhere?'

'It was a gift from Noah, Mummy.'

'I'm not stupid. You buy it yourself, not Noah,' her mother retorted as she shut the door.

Chapter 2

The lunchtime crowd was noisier than usual. Saloma looked up and noticed a group of young office workers seated at a big table, taking selfies and chatting above the noise. It must be someone's birthday, Saloma thought. She took a sip of water and listened with half an ear to the conversation between Su-Ann and Janice.

'Sal? Are you listening?' Su-Ann piped up as she leaned forward, nearly knocking down her glass of ice lemon tea.

'Yes, of course. I'm sorry, I was distracted by the noise. It's very loud in here.'

'I like it. I think this place has a great vibe,' Su-Ann declared, as she looked around her with pleasure. 'And this . . .this fried calamari is to die for!' she said as she took a bite. 'Thanks for getting us a table,' she said with her mouth full, 'I know that there's a long waiting list. You and your connections!'

'I just happened to know the owner, that's all,' Saloma said, with a slight lift of her shoulder.

'Just happened? You said it so casually! You probably have him on speed dial while mere mortals like us have our kids' private tutors on ours!'

Saloma gave a faint smile.

'Is your salmon to your liking?' Su-Ann asked, her fork suspended in the air.

'What? Yes, of course. I'm just not very hungry.'

'If I had your figure, I would have ordered the pasta and *dessert!* Honestly, Sal, you look amazing! When you walked in, all the diners gawked at you.'

'That's true. I noticed it too,' Janice said, as she nibbled on some lettuce.

'And the short hair suits you! It shows off your beautiful bone structure. You know, you're a puzzle.'

'What do you mean?' Saloma asked.

'I mean, just look at you,' Su-Ann said, as she held out her hands at Saloma.

'You're so tall and exotic but I have to say that you're not as . . . I mean, not as pigmented as the rest of your race. Have you thought of finding out your genealogy?'

'Not as pigmented?' Saloma asked, eyebrow raised.

'Well, you know what I mean! You're just not as tanned, like let me see,' Su-Ann said, staring into space. 'You're like an almond while the rest of your race are like cinnamon or coffee. Not that it's bad,' Su-Ann hastened to add. 'As I was saying, you can do a DNA test or get a professional genealogist to help you. You must do your family tree first, of course,' she continued unabated.

Saloma placed her fork down and thought for a moment. 'As a matter of fact, my mother and her relatives *did* a fair bit of research on their family's background.'

'So, what did they find?' Su-Ann asked, as she leaned forward with her arms on the table, her eyes fixed on Saloma.

'Well, apparently, she, I mean my mother,' Saloma said, to which Su-Ann and Janice nodded impatiently, 'is a direct descendent of a prince from Sumatra.'

'I knew it! He must be a mix of Indonesian and Dutch,' Su-Ann exclaimed, putting her fork down with a clatter.

'And, what else,' Janice asked, throwing an irritated look at Su-Ann.

'Well,' Saloma said, as she leaned against her chair and picked out a thread on her blouse. 'This Prince came to Negri Sembilan, Malaysia as you know,' Saloma added to the two earnest faces looking at her, 'fell in love with one of the locals and gave up his throne.'

Janice gasped.

'He gave it all up,' Su-Ann whispered.

Saloma nodded. 'He gave up all his princely duties, his wealth and married a commoner,' Saloma finished, dabbing her lips with a napkin.

'What a story! Do you know what he did after he married her? Did he become rich again? This is like King Edward who gave up everything for his wife!' Su-Ann said, looking at Saloma with excitement.

Saloma shrugged. 'Hardly similar. I think *my* prince,' Saloma said with a small smile, 'just became like one of the villagers and lived there till he died.'

'I'm sure he was tall, with good bone structure even if he wasn't rich. You definitely have Dutch blood in you!' Su-Ann declared. 'And on top of that, you're educated and eloquent!'

Saloma paused and drew circles on the tablecloth with her forefinger, weighing the words she was about to say.

'Su-Ann, what's this obsession with colour and race?'

Su-Ann looked at Saloma, her face bright red under her make-up.

'What do you mean, Sal? We're just talking about your genealogy.'

'Exactly, why did you ask mine and not Janice's?'

'Well, I don't know what to say Sal. I guess cos she's Chinese like me, so there's not much mystery in there. Sorry, Janice,' Su-Ann said, turning to her.

Janice nodded, looking anywhere but at Saloma.

'We've been friends for a long time, and I think I can be honest?' Saloma asked, glancing at both though Janice was studying her napkin.

'Of course,' Su-Ann said, her voice barely a whisper.

'Su-Ann, you've been talking about my race specifically and the various shades of my people. It seems to be a topic that many people in this country just talk about with such casual ease, but honestly, it's hard when you're at the receiving end. It's not like I can change the colour of my skin. I've struggled with this all my life, and in a way, I have come to accept it but it's especially hard when friends do it too. I mean we come in all different shapes, sizes, and colours but of the three, colour seems to be front and centre.' Saloma held up her hand when Su-Ann tried to speak, 'Please let me finish.' Saloma took a deep breath. 'Su-Ann, you said that I'm lighter skinned than the rest of my race, you mentioned that I'm almond while the rest are cinnamon and coffee. *So*, does that mean that you won't be friends with me if I turned a few shades darker? Or will we be tighter friends if conversely, I became a few shades lighter by some force of miracle? Will I be more acceptable? And why did you assume that I must have Dutch blood and not some other race? The Malays came from Borneo and moved to Sumatra and the Malay Peninsula due to trade and sea activities. They spoke a variety of dialects and came in various shades of brown. In Singapore, we are lumped as one as we speak the same language.'

'Sal, I'm truly sorry,' Su-Ann whispered. 'I honestly didn't mean any offence. I was actually paying you a compliment.'

'But that is the point. It wasn't a compliment. Look, guys, I'm sorry, this has made you uncomfortable,' Saloma said. 'And the sad part is that even my own race has turned on us; those of us who are, as you said, coffee coloured.'

Su-Ann winced and Saloma reached out to pat her hand.

'I just got an earful from my mother earlier. She asked whether I've been out in the sun longer than usual. See, we get it from both sides,' Saloma said, with a grin.

'I'm really sorry, Sal. I know you're trying to make light of it now. You've held a mirror in front of me, rightfully so, and I honestly feel bad, ashamed even. This is after all, the twenty-first century, I should have known better. I've never tried to look at it from your point of view and that is on me. I'm truly sorry.'

'I appreciate your honesty too,' Saloma said, reaching for Su-Ann hands and gripping them tight.

Janice reached out and placed her hands on top of theirs and Saloma burst out laughing.

'Look at us, sad middle-aged women!'

Su-Ann wiped her eyes and said, 'Saloma, in all honesty, you're beautiful, articulate, and successful even if you suddenly turn purple!'

Saloma laughed. 'Okay, that's way too much but thank you!'

'Come to think of it, as teachers, we should be eloquent like you, but it makes things so much easier when we lapse into Singlish especially when we speak to the kids' parents. Are those bling-bling yours?' Su-Ann asked suddenly.

'Honestly, Su-Ann, you change subjects so randomly,' Janice burst out.

Saloma looked at Janice's indignant face and laughed.

'These?' Saloma asked as she fingered the diamond studs on her ears to which Su-Ann nodded. 'Yup, they're mine. Technically they're my mother's. I remodelled her diamond rings into these. See, this link,' Saloma said, leaning closer to Su-Ann and showing a part of her earring, 'This is from her ring. I kept them and refashioned them into this modern look.'

'How amazing!' Su-Ann declared. 'That's such a great idea. So, if I pass you my wedding pieces, you can make them into something current?'

'Absolutely!' Saloma said. 'That's the whole concept of my line.'

'I wish I could have piercings. You have three on each lobe, right?' Su-Ann asked, peering closer. 'You wear your jewellery exquisitely. I would love to go to your boutique. Can we have a discount?' Su-Ann asked.

'Yes, can we?' Janice asked, tentatively.

'Of course. Not a problem but you'll have to wait. My atelier is not launched yet. But soon,' Saloma said.

'You girls have been too kind. As for my figure, it's just genes, exercise, and good food. That's all. It's not rocket science.'

'May not be rocket science, but it's not a regimen for the faint hearted. After my second child, I just ballooned,' Su-Ann said, blowing her cheeks. 'But Janice, you're just as skinny,' Su-Ann said, giving Janice a thorough run-down. 'You haven't changed a bit since our school days.'

'I just can't put on weight. Even during pregnancy,' Janice said.

'I wish *I* had that problem!' Su-Ann laughed.

'So, Su-Ann,' Saloma asked, moving her food around her plate, 'You mentioned that you're going to quit teaching?'

'Yes, my oldest boy will be sitting for his O-Levels next year. He's so playful, if I left him to his own devices, he'll fail. Aren't you glad that you don't have to go through this, Sal?'

'What? Oh, children are not for Noah and me. Our businesses are our babies! Trust me, they can be as exhausting and draining but of course, being a parent must be something altogether different!'

'It's tiring for sure, but the joy is priceless. Despite all my complaints, being a mother is *the* best role for me,' Su-Ann gushed.

'Good for you,' Saloma said.

'Why did you marry if you don't want to have children, Sal?' Janice asked with quiet diffidence.

'Why? Well, why not?' Saloma replied with a frown. 'We love each other, and want to commit to each other, just like anybody else. And we want a certificate to prove that. I don't think marriage is all about having children,' Saloma said, with honesty. 'I don't think, or we don't feel that having children is something one must do in life. It's a huge responsibility. I think it's terrible to have kids and then live to regret it. Noah and me just want to focus on our dreams, enjoy each other's company, travel, and grow old together,' Saloma said, with a slight shrug.

Janice nodded. 'I get it. You and Noah are so honest with each other. I don't think I have had such deep and meaningful discussions with my husband. Most of the time, we talk about the kids, school, and food, and in that order too!'

Saloma and Su-Ann looked at each other and roared with laughter.

'That's the most we've heard from you, girl! Half the time, you're quiet as a mouse!' Su-Ann declared.

Janice giggled. 'Back to the topic of your son, Su-Ann, isn't he in one of the top schools?'

'Yes, but that's not enough. He needs coaching and tuition. That was how I found you, Sal. I was looking around for good tuition agencies and your husband's tuition agency came highly recommended. In fact, it was one of the teachers who mentioned you.'

'It's actually my husband's business, *his* baby,' Saloma said, tongue in cheek. 'But then, what's the difference, his money is your money, and your money is your money! Right ladies?'

'I don't know about that. Richard handles all our finances,' Janice said.

'Actually, Jong does it too.' Su-Ann said.

'But you have a job, Su-Ann. Surely, you have your own account?' Saloma asked, stirring her coffee.

'I don't. Everything goes into our joint account. But it's okay, it's not like he's going to run away with it! And he's better with numbers than me. I have no clue about insurance and investments. Anyway, I have my hands full with my two boys!' Su-Ann said with a chuckle.

'Well, I'm not working, nor contributing, so I *definitely* don't have an account of my own. I'm just like Su-Ann, my two girls take up all of my time,' Janice said, with surprising honesty.

'But girls, isn't it important to know our finances? Or all aspects of our marriage to be precise. We have to be smarter than our mothers,' Saloma declared.

'But Richard is the sole breadwinner. He decides if we have enough for a holiday, or it's time to get a new car, so on and so forth. I don't think I have the right to handle the finances or make financial suggestions. It's his money. He gives me an allowance every month, for the upkeep of the house, the kids, and if there's some balance, I treat myself to a day at the spa or get something nice for myself. It's a step up from my mother, that's for sure. She didn't even get an allowance,' Janice said. 'I thought all marriages are like that, like Richard and me?' Janice said, glancing at Saloma and Su-Ann.

Saloma stared at Janice for a full second. 'How about you, Su-Ann?' Saloma asked.

'Um, we have a joint account as I said earlier. That's the only one we have. But then, come to think of it, I wouldn't have a clue if he had opened another one or several for that matter,' Su-Ann said with a frown. Her brow cleared. 'It's all right. Even if he did, it's for the good of the family,' she said, taking a spoonful of her tiramisu. 'But Saloma, you couldn't possibly know Noah's business? You did say that it's his baby,' Su-Ann said.

'I do, in fact. I handle all the accounts of our two businesses. Of course, we have an accountant, but he reports to me and Noah,

as and when. In fact, sometimes, I even give Noah an allowance,'
Saloma said with a chuckle.

'Oh,' Su-Ann said, as she and Janice exchanged looks of
mutual surprise. 'All this money talk is boring. Tell us more about
yourself, Sal? Like how's your Mum, Aunty Marina. We haven't
seen her in years. Does she still cook? I can still remember her *nasi
lemak*. Her *sambal* was legendary! I hope you got her recipe, Sal,'
Su-Ann said, as she took a sip of her cocktail.

'Oh, she's fine. Busy with her own friends,' Saloma said as she
signalled the waitress for the bill.

'Are you leaving?' Janice asked, as the waitress handed
Saloma the bill.

'I'm afraid so, girls. It was good catching up. Let's do this
again,' Saloma said as she stood up.

'Hey, wait a minute. Split the bill and tell us our share,' Janice
said, putting a hand on Saloma's wrist.

'No worries. It's on me,' Saloma said with a wink and a wave.

Chapter 3

Saloma straightened her body and surveyed the large expanse of her living room. The floor to ceiling windows reminded her of the window displays of the boutiques in London and New York, except no one could press their faces against the clear glazed glass to peer in. The real estate agent hadn't been lying when he first told her that the apartment was like a cocoon, far removed from the city below with its daily grind. In fact, she liked to think she was in the same space as the birds that whizzed past and occasionally perched on the outdoor balcony that ran along the house.

Her eyes rested on the pigmented resin painting that occupied almost the whole wall of her living room. Sunlight shone unerringly on it making it even more fluidlike. She walked towards it, her bare feet cool under the marble flooring. Unconsciously, she reached out her hand to touch the abstract elements in vivid cyan, magenta, yellow, and black. The moment her fingers grazed the painting, she dropped her hand and stepped back to study it again.

'You're back,' a voice called out.

Saloma turned around and smiled at Noah who was standing in the middle of the living room, his hands deep in his trousers pockets.

'Noah, I didn't hear you come in,' she said. 'Don't you love this painting? It has an inexplicable magnetic pull, it draws you in, without fail, no matter how many times you look at it,' Saloma said, staring at it again. 'It was a beautiful trip, wasn't it?'

'Beautiful trip?'

'Yes, the trip we made to Bandung in 2005,' Saloma said, looking up at Noah. 'The BMW Sotheby Art Tour where we met several artists including Arin. He was so much younger then. Now, he's famous. As he should be. I was told this painting would fetch a good price today, not that I want to part with it. Do you remember, Pak Hartono?' Saloma asked, as she looked at him enquiringly.

'The banker?'

'Yes, he and his family were just as keen to get the painting and it was so fun to see who would get it in the end! Thanks for buying it for me,' Saloma said.

Noah shrugged. 'Hmm. Aren't you going to get dressed?' he asked, changing the subject as he rocked on his heels.

'What? Oh yes, in a minute. We still have time,' Saloma said as she inspected the vases on the coffee table. 'The part-time servers are in the kitchen, getting everything prepped and I even called Happy, in case I need a pair of extra hands,' she said, as she rearranged the flowers.

'Yes, I noticed. I saw her in the dining room. I think she was giving a stern briefing to the servers.'

Saloma smiled. 'Yes, that's Happy all right, I know she will carry out my instructions to the letter.'

'Why don't you just hire her permanently? By the way, is that her real name?'

'Um no, I won't hire her permanently. We're good this way. She's too much for me full time. And yes, that *is* her real name. It seemed that she was a happy baby,' Saloma said, as she stood back to study her handiwork.

'All right, I'll head to the study to make a few calls and I'll see you in the foyer at seven,' Noah said as he turned on his heel.

'Wait, Noah! I didn't get to see your outfit,' Saloma said, turning round to face him fully. 'You're wearing the Etro shirt I got you! You always look good in white,' she said, as she straightened the collar.

'Kind of hard not to since you laid it out on the bed.'

Saloma giggled.

'Um, thanks for getting this amazing apartment for us, Noah and for throwing this housewarming party,' Saloma whispered. 'I know you prefer our previous home, but this location is just perfect. *Just perfect.* We're close to everything. No more rushing in the mornings,' she said, linking her arms around his neck.

Noah raised an eyebrow and unlinked her arms. 'Well, you did choose the apartment *and* arrange the party.'

'Who me?' Saloma asked in mock surprise as she darted to the bedroom to change.

Chapter 4

'Where's that talented wife of yours, Noah? I must tell her that this spread of hers is absolutely brilliant! How does she do it? We need to market this skill of hers!'

'Hi Karl, she's over there with . . .' Noah said, his voice trailing off. He caught Saloma's eyes and shrugged.

'Don't bother Noah, I see her!' Karl said, as he weaved his way towards Saloma. 'Hey, Sal, I'm loving this canapé party of yours! What a great idea. Who would have thought these small morsels could be so delightful.'

'Hi Karl,' Saloma said as she excused herself from a group of women and steered Karl to the side of the room.

'I'm glad you like it. I've always wanted to make an hors d'oeuvre party and this is a perfect opportunity,' Saloma said, tucking her hair behind her ear.

'But the amount of work involved must have been staggering,' Karl said, his naked head glistened under the artificial light, save for the snowy wreath of hair around the sides of his head.

Saloma laughed. 'That's true but it pays to know that my guests, like you, appreciate it.'

'I love everything you made, the *rendang* with the brioche, the sambal prawns with the croissant, the fried bananas. They're all *heavenly*,' he emphasized, rolling his eyes in. 'You do know that I've a string of restaurants and a nose for spotting trends? I opened my first in London's Shoreditch neighbourhood long before it was considered hip and in Singapore's Dempsey Road when you locals still thought it was a place to hunt for used furniture.'

'Of course I do, silly,' Saloma said with a smile.

'You know that I've always loved Malay cuisine in Singapore. Many people tend to forget the complexity involved in the making of one dish, the sambal for instance, takes patience and care, as it must have just the right proportion of sweet, sour, spiciness, and of course the umami flavour from the shrimp paste.'

'Well done, Karl,' Saloma said. 'For an Englishman, you certainly know your way around our food.'

'So, let's open a fine dining Malay restaurant. We can have starters like what you have here and move on to mains with a modern twist. It will be a hit, with you at the helm.'

Saloma pursed her lips. 'In theory, this sounds really wonderful. But it's hard to make my food fine dining as our ingredients are not as pricey as, say the Chinese for instance. They can charge premium prices for their hairy crabs, shark's fin, abalone, just to name a few. We can't exactly do the same.'

'Don't put down your culture, Saloma! It's rich and vibrant. You just need to market it right. C'mon, the Italians for example, have fine dining restaurants and their pastas and pizzas are not exactly complex.'

'Yes, the Italians have certainly taken over the world. But I've seen several Malay chefs open high-end Malay restaurant only to have it close down a couple of years later. Diners just can't accept paying such high prices, even in glamorous settings, when they can get equally good food at the hawker centres. Maybe, if I open one in Europe, I can justify the prices.'

'Then it's sorted! We can have one in London. I'll call my office and we can have a discussion.'

Saloma held up her hand.

'Before you go further, I know what you're going to say and the answer is still no, Karl. Believe me, I'm flattered but I can only cook for people that I care for, I can't do it for strangers.'

'All right, all right. You've made your case often enough. It's just that I'm a businessman and this is just too good to pass!'

'Excuse me. Saloma, this is a lovely apartment!'

'Sheeny! Lovely to see you. Thank you for accepting my invitation,' Saloma said, bending down to hug her guest. 'I'm sorry, Karl, can you excuse me,' Saloma said, turning to Karl.

'Of course! You know my number if you ever change your mind,' Karl said, wiping his head with a napkin.

'I will, promise.'

'I'll go and see if there's any food left,' he said with a wink and ambled over to the buffet table.

'What was that about?' Sheeny asked, her crimson lips parting to show perfect veneers.

'Oh, nothing,' Saloma said with a laugh.

'This is a beautiful apartment and it's so spacious! Honestly, you can fit scores of people in that outdoor balcony of yours!' Sheeny said, looking around her.

'I don't think so, Sheeny, but thank you. Would you like a tour?'

'Your distinguished husband has given me a tour. He's such a gentleman, so attentive and gracious. Is he always like that?'

Saloma burst out laughing.

'He's more of a listener than a talker. I'm the one who chats non-stop.'

'Is Noah a Singaporean?'

'Yes, born and bred. His family originated from northern India and there is some European ancestry, so I guess, that explains his height,' Saloma said, waving at a familiar face across the room. Her eyes caught sight of Noah and she paused. He was standing next to a woman whose back was facing Saloma and she couldn't quite place who she was. He bent down to hear her better and his face creased into a smile at something she said.

'Saloma?'

Saloma smiled and turned her attention to Sheeny. 'My apologies. Can you repeat what you just said?'

'I said that Noah is more than just tall, he can pass off as a movie star!'

'I will tell him that! That will make him laugh.'

'And you? Is your family here?'

'I'm a Singaporean too, Sheeny!' Saloma said, taking a sip of her bubbly water.

'I meant, are your parents here?' Sheeny asked, looking around.

Saloma took her time to take another sip of water.

'Um, no. My father has passed and my mother isn't here.'

'I see. And are you going to fill this lovely home of yours with beautiful children?' Sheeny asked, looking at Saloma with a curious eye.

'Sheeny, we have passed our prime! No babies for us!'

'But the two of you are so young!'

'Well, according to nature we've passed our expiration dates! Excuse me, Sheeny, I can see my helper calling me,' Saloma said, with a fixed smile and made her way to the kitchen. She caught sight of Noah in the mirror and this time, he was with a couple of ladies from their apartment building. She couldn't remember the last time she had seen him so relaxed and comfortable.

'Ma'am, come to the kitchen,' Happy whispered.

'All right, what's the problem?' Saloma asked, puzzled.

'I'll tell you in the kitchen, ma'am. Come.'

'Happy, what are you doing?' Saloma whispered as she allowed the four-foot-tall, middle-aged woman to steer her to the kitchen.

'In here, ma'am,' Happy said, as she weaved through the kitchen, deftly avoiding the servers in black suits, with their white gloved hands holding trays of food and drinks.

'For goodness' sake, Happy!' Saloma said, all too aware of her stilettos clacking on the tiled kitchen floor.

'Look at these!' Happy said, stopping suddenly and causing Saloma to bump into her.

Saloma eyed an array of hampers in varying sizes on the kitchen counters. They were all opened with the ribbons and wrappers pushed to one side.

'What about them?' Saloma asked, annoyed.

'Ma'am, Madam Sheeny's driver just brought them in. He said, housewarming present from Madam Sheeny.'

'All right. Just unpack them and keep them in the pantry,' Saloma said, turning to leave.

'Ma'am, wait,' Happy said, her small fingers clutching Saloma's wrist. 'I know you said to put in pantry but I don't know what to do now.'

Saloma looked down at the familiar round chin and low hairline and tried to make sense of the situation.

'Happy, just tell me.'

'Many expired, ma'am! Expired last year. Look,' Happy said as she picked up a tin of abalone. 'See, it says here, expired last year. And this,' Happy said, as she lifted a basket of cosmetics, 'One or two can use but many cannot!'

Saloma eyed the colourful assortment of designer eyeshadows and blushers, their famous logos emblazoned across the covers. She picked one up and turned it in the palm of her hand. True enough, the expiration date was way off the mark. She opened it and brought it to her nose. 'Ugh. Throw it away. All of them. Pack them discreetly and bring them downstairs to the bins.'

'This not first time, ma'am. I know her helper. We meet always on Sundays. She said Madam Sheeny is very bad, very stingy. She gives people presents from other people and sometimes, she asked her driver to,' Happy lowered her voice, 'to get free food at the temples and give them to her staff: her two helpers and assistant.' Happy looked behind her to make sure that no one was listening.

'Just throw them away, Happy.' Saloma strode out of the kitchen, making a mental note not to invite Sheeny again.

Chapter 5

Saloma lathered her arms and legs with lotion, massaging it deeply into her long limbs. She felt better after taking a shower. Karl had been the last one to leave at two in the morning, drunk and incoherent. Noah had picked him up under his armpits and dragged him to his waiting driver at the lobby.

She sat on her vanity chair and reached for her skin-lightening night moisturizer, applying the thick dollop of cream generously onto her bare face. Her fingers worked the cream into her face, before moving to her neck and chest. She stared into the eye of her own reflection: the clear, tanned skin, taut over her high cheeks and jawline, the almond-shaped eyes upturned at the ends under trimmed, arched eyebrows, the straight nose, and her wide, full lips which Noah claimed were his favourite feature, other than her legs. She smiled at the thought. But then, wasn't it common for a man to make comments on a woman's body? She recalled many occasions at work, where her male colleagues made innuendoes about the women in her department, sometimes even grading them from a high of ten to a low of one. It had incensed her when they appeared unmoved when chastised, claiming it was all done in good fun.

She walked out into the living room, her footsteps muffled by her bedroom slippers.

'Noah? Are you out here?' Finding the outdoor balcony door open, she peered outside and saw him lying on a deck chair, staring at the city skyline lighting up the otherwise dark night. He hadn't changed though he had untucked his shirt, and a bottle of water was on the floor, next to him. Saloma pulled a chair closer to him and sat alongside him, and despite the closeness, she knew that he was miles away.

'We could see Johor from up here,' she said.

Noah took a sip of his water and stretched out his legs, placing his hands behind his head. 'You've said that before. It was on your list of ten reasons why we should get the apartment.'

'I think the exact words I said were: "The view is spectacular. We could even see Johor from the distance,"' Saloma said, turning to face his profile. 'Are you regretting our purchase?'

Noah shrugged and closed his eyes.

'I know you'll come to love this place, Noah. In time, you'll love it as much as our old home, your family home.'

Saloma slid lower into her chair and crossed her legs at the ankles, studying her bunny slippers. 'I think the housewarming party was a success. Everyone seemed to have a good time. What do you think?'

'You're a good host. You made sure that everyone had a good time.'

'What was that? A backhanded compliment?'

Noah opened one eye and looked at her. 'Just that. You're a good host.'

Saloma shifted in her seat and made herself more comfortable. 'Um, who was the lady you were talking to earlier? The one in the black dress.'

'Sal, almost all the ladies wore black or some dark colour or other. I can't possibly remember,' Noah said, his eyes still closed.

'That's fair. I couldn't see her face, hence, I mentioned the dress. I don't think I invited her,' Saloma said.

'That's strange. If you couldn't see her face, how would you know who she was?'

Saloma sat up. 'Noah, I was just wondering that's all. You were laughing.' She reached for his hand and placed his palm against her cheek. 'I haven't seen you laugh for a long time. That's all.'

Noah took his hand away and rubbed his jaw. 'I can't remember, Sal. Maybe it was Khim, one of our new teachers. She shared with me something funny that happened in her class, and it was nice, it was nice to hear about the kids.'

'Oh, I don't remember inviting her,' Saloma said, with a frown.

'Wait what?' Noah said, sitting up. 'Are you saying that I have to go through you?'

'No, of course not! I just assumed that you left such things to me,' Saloma replied with haste.

'But that's your problem, isn't it? Making assumptions,' Noah said, leaning back again.

Saloma cleared her throat and modulated her voice to be soft. 'I'm sorry, Noah. It's my fault. Of course, you have every right to invite anyone to our home. I just thought you looked relaxed and happy at the party. It was good to see that. I missed that. Speaking of which, Lee cornered me at the end of the evening and brought up his idea again of opening a premium preschool, from nursery to kindergarten. He found a good location and was hoping we could meet up with his people. I think it's a fantastic development!'

Saloma turned on her side and faced his motionless figure.

'Noah, Lee doesn't just meet *anybody*. He is a well-known developer in Asia. His team is made up of famous architects, designers, and contractors. And for *him* and not his staff, mind you, to make time to come to our housewarming says something about *you*, the success of *your* tuition centres, and this phenomenal opportunity. *Now* is the time for *us*, Noah. Imagine what we can do if this venture turns out successful? The recognition, the acceptance. It's priceless.' Saloma reached out to touch his hand that lay closest to her. 'You've made a name for yourself and this is the reward! Your centres are island-wide and there is still a long list of children waiting to get in. Noah, people that I've lost touch with are contacting me through social media, begging me to get their kids to your centres! Imagine that, Noah. Classmates who used to ignore me at school are now contacting me, asking me to register their kids. How far you've come. From an ordinary school teacher to this! An entrepreneur.'

Noah stared at the darkened sky.

'You *do* know that I don't have training or experience in early childhood education,' Noah eventually spoke.

'Don't you see, that's the beauty of it! You don't need to! We will employ the very best in the business. In fact, Lee has shortlisted a few candidates. That would not be an issue,' Saloma said, tightening her grip on his arm. 'Noah, your name has become larger than life, and we will ensure that the standards of the school are the same as how you run the centres.'

'Who's the "we" you're talking about?' Noah asked, still staring at the sky.

'I'm sorry, *sayang*, I meant Lee, me, and hopefully, you too,' Saloma said, with a nervous laugh.

'What about your jewellery business?'

'What about it?'

'If we agree to this craziness, you'd have less time to focus on your own business, don't you have a new line coming up or an open house? I can't quite remember which.'

Saloma laughed. 'It's sweet of you to think of me but I can handle both. And at the moment, it's just discussions with Lee. Nothing concrete. It doesn't harm just to listen to him.'

Noah emptied the bottle of water with one gulp. 'I love teaching, Sal. It was simpler back then.'

Saloma leaned towards him. 'And you still can teach if you want to! Just go to one of the centres and take over a few classes. Parents will be thrilled if you did that. Word will get around.

Noah Salem is back at work, casting a spell on the kids. I can just see that happening!'

Noah stood up and picked up his shoes. 'It's not the same, Sal. And not everything has to be for publicity, for optics.'

Saloma stood up too and stopped him in his tracks. 'I was kidding, you know that. But not about the teaching. You can still do that. Look, if you don't want to meet Lee, I can do it on my own. I'll attend all the boring meetings, discussions and I'll keep you posted. If you feel that it's not worthwhile, I'll let him know. No biggie.'

'As you wish, Sal,' he said, stepping away.

Saloma watched as he walked away and bit her lip. It was time to call Mavis again.

Chapter 6

Singapore 2000s

As the train pulled into Orchard MRT station, Saloma looked up from her seat and saw a familiar figure standing at the platform. Her eyes widened. It couldn't be. She craned her neck to get a better look as the train slowed down. It was him: the squared set of his shoulders, the prominent forehead, and his unmistakable stance of standing almost like a soldier, at attention. He was dressed in a white t-shirt over a pair of faded blue jeans, with a black sports bag slung over one shoulder. He still wore his flaxen hair cropped close to his skull but with a short fringe. A jolt of adrenaline shot through her as she watched him step onto the train. She didn't dare move. The last time she saw him was when they collected their A-Level results at school. Not that it mattered. In the entire two years of college, he had barely glanced her way. But who could blame him? His Asian and European ancestry gave him a physical appeal that was hard to ignore and had made him popular.

Saloma looked around the cabin, it was empty, except for an elderly couple who hardly exchanged a word to each other. She uncrossed her legs and balanced the three files on her lap, pulling down her denim skirt to cover her thighs. He couldn't have seen her and even if he did, she was sure he wouldn't remember. The train doors closed and Saloma leaned back against the window with her eyes shut. Her heart was still racing.

'Saloma? It's you, isn't?' a male voice called out, his accent neutral.

Her eyes flew open and she found him standing in front of her. His eyes were light brown, with flecks of gold. She cleared her throat and nodded.

'I'm Noah. Noah Salem. We were in junior college together, if you could remember,' he said. The train jerked, and he lurched forward, saved by the grab handle. He burst out laughing, the sound warm and easy-going. 'May I?' he asked, pointing at the empty seat next to hers.

'Oh, of course, please.'

He folded his long length next to her and placed his bag between his legs. 'How long has it been? Ten years?' he asked, turning around to face her.

Saloma gripped her hands together, 'Yes, I think so.'

He shook his head and leaned back against the window. 'Man, that was a whole different life. We were not in the same class, as I recall. You were in A11?'

Saloma arranged the files on her lap and nodded her head.

'You look great.'

Saloma noticed his eyes graze over her bare legs.

'But then, you always have.'

Saloma raised an eyebrow.

'We had a list, the top ten girls we would like to date, and you made it to the top five. Yes, it's true,' he repeated to the derisive look in her eyes. 'Well, we didn't actually had the guts to approach you girls. Damn, all of you were so aloof. None of us had the courage to step up. So, we just appreciated from a distance,' he said with a laugh. 'I must tell this to my kids. They would have a good laugh.'

'Kids?' Saloma whispered.

Noah smiled, his eyes crinkled in the corners, making him seem a little older than his twenty-eight years. 'Not my biological kids. Just my students.'

Saloma frowned.

'I'm a teacher. Have been since graduation. Found my calling.'

'You are? I never would have guessed.'

Noah leaned forward, his hands between his legs.

'Why do people always say that? Anyway, how are you?' He eyed the folders on her lap. 'Work?'

Saloma shrugged. 'Oh, I have a presentation to do, and these are just some of the materials I need to go through. I'm on a three-day course, and it ended early which gives me time to prepare for tomorrow.'

Noah nodded. 'You're with private sector or a struggling civil servant like me?'

Saloma grimaced. 'Public sector. My Dad had drummed into my head from the moment I got into University: "Sal, you must get a stable job, an iron-clad one after your graduation,"' Saloma said, mimicking her father's gruff voice.

'Ah, your father must have been a civil servant too.'

Saloma gave him a quick nod. She looked at his faded jeans. Up close, they were threadbare and torn at some parts. 'Casual Wednesday?'

He chuckled. 'I'm in charge of the school's football team. We had a game earlier. I had to get out of my sports gear. This was all I had. By the way, where are you alighting?' he asked, looking up at the train map across the aisle.

'Um, the next one, in fact. Ang Mo Kio.'

'Give me your number and we can arrange to meet up?'

Saloma looked around and found a few of the passengers looking at her with interest. She cleared her throat. 'Um, I don't have paper.'

'Sure you do. Just tear a small piece from your notes.'

Saloma open her folder, her face suffused with heat. She tore a corner piece, scribbled her number, and slipped it into the palm of his hand. 'This is my stop,' she said as she scrambled up and made her way to the exit. 'See ya,' she said over her shoulder, fully aware that he would never call her. He probably had a different girl every week. Anyway, good looking men like him don't go after her, right?

But two days later on a Friday evening, she found herself staring at the floor blankly, wondering whether the call was all in her head.

'Sal, telephone ring? Who call?' her mother called out from the kitchen. 'Sal?'

Saloma looked up and found her mother standing in front of her, her hair screwed up at the back of her head, tapping a wooden ladle against her thigh.

'Um, yes, Mummy?'

'What is wrong with you? I ask who call?'

'Um, just an old classmate. He invited me for lunch on Sunday,' Saloma said, not quite believing the words she just uttered.

Her mother's hand stilled. The ladle, yellowed with turmeric stains stood out against her black batik *sarong*. 'He?'

'Um, what?' Saloma caught her mother's wide-eyed stare. Even in her faded, flower-patterned blouse and her washed out sarong, she looked a good twenty years younger than her age. The white patches on her face and body had spread evenly over the years, giving her a strangely brand-new skin: one that was lighter, softer and unblemished. Even the dermatologist who had attended her mother for years, was surprised at the transformation. His eyes had darted back and forth between Saloma and her mother, as if he was at a tennis match. 'Madam Marina, people will mistake you as Chinese or even Eurasian now! Your skin is like the colour of tofu.' Her mother had giggled like a silly schoolgirl but his comment had stung Saloma.

'Yes, it was a guy, Mummy,' Saloma finally answered. 'We were in junior college together. We just happened to meet . . . just recently.'

'You like someone? Finally. You never go out. What is it? A date?' her mother asked, looking at Saloma for confirmation. 'Me at your age, already a mother.'

Saloma expelled her breath and tried to quell her rising annoyance. 'I know, Mummy. You've told me a million times when you got married, got pregnant. As for this guy, he was in college with me . . . I just met him, Mummy. It's hardly a date. We're just going to catch up this weekend. He's not about to propose to me,' she said with a big laugh. 'Let me save you the trouble, *nothing* is going to happen. I'm not his type.'

'You too fussy. Always meet men not your race. Your father to blame. He speak English, read English books. Everything English. Make you forget where you come from. Many Malay boys like you. My friend, Endang, example. She said, her son like you. Every time I go market, she there telling me, "My son, Razak, like Sal. Give me her office number. Is it a secret?" But I cannot give. You don't allow. Very bad for me. Now, I hide when I see her,' her mother said, raising her voice.

Saloma stood up.

'Now what? Every time we talk this topic, you run.'

It was true. She loathed to talk to her mother about the men she was dating. Maybe it was time to speak the truth. She sat down with a bump on the arm of the sofa.

'Mummy, please sit down. You're like a crazy person, standing there with a ladle, shouting at me.'

Her mother looked down at herself and took a seat at the edge of the sofa. 'I no shouting. You so rude, calling me crazy.'

'I didn't mean it like that. I'm sorry.' Saloma lowered her voice and sat next to her.

'Mummy, I like to meet people from different backgrounds. Get to know different cultures.'

'You talking rubbish!' her mother exclaimed, her round eyes shining in disbelief. 'You think I stupid. Blind? You not care about other people's culture!'

'Okay, maybe I'm not *that* interested,' Saloma admitted, her face flushed. 'But even when I'm dating men outside my race, well . . . to be honest, sometimes it's like walking on a minefield. They find me educated and fun, but that's it. It stops there. I feel I'm not good enough as a girlfriend or a wife. I don't know,' Saloma's voice trailed off.

'So, meet Malay men. Simple. Easy.'

'Trust me, Mummy, I have. There was this one guy, he was nice enough. He was educated, spoke well, and was fine, I guess.' Saloma shrugged. 'But he didn't like it when I spoke my mind, especially in a crowd. So, even though, he was educated, he still preferred women to be submissive. He also mentioned that he wanted a stay-at-home wife and to continue living with his parents.'

'That's okay, I see no problem.'

'Really, Mummy. Even you and Pa lived on your own when you got married,' Saloma shot back.

'You arrogant. You think you too good for Malay men,' her mother finished with a snort.

Saloma averted her gaze and studied her hands. 'Mummy, you got it all wrong. I'm not accepted by both types of men, but between the two groups, I must say that, it's easier to communicate with men outside my race. Most of these Malay men you talked about or that I have met, they . . . I'm sorry to say this, but I make more money than them. And . . . um, I'm sure they're good men,' Saloma hastened to add when her mother raised her eyebrows, 'but many of them are not interested in higher learning. Which is their choice, of course, but education matters to me. I want someone who is an intellectual. We just have different goals.'

'And also,' Saloma hesitated, 'they're all shorter than me.'

'You forget about Halim. He tall. Got car. Still you don't' like!'

'Okay, he had a car but that's because he was older than me, and had worked longer, saved more. Good for him. But we had nothing in common. He didn't like to read or be curious about the world or people. He was um . . . a little boring actually,' Saloma replied. Her mother sat unmoved, a dark look in her eyes. Saloma closed her eyes and gave herself a couple of minutes before she excused herself to her room.

'So Sal, all not good for you? This is what you say,' her mother retorted. She leaned forward and peered into Saloma's face, 'Sal, *all* men the same. Brown, white, yellow, black. Tall, short. Fat, thin. Education. No education. No matter. All want same things. But marry someone our race is *easier*. He understands our culture. One day you know. Just pick one. One who is happy to take care of you. You getting old. Don't wait until *no one* wants you!'

Saloma stared at her mother. 'That's your advice?'

Her mother stood up and made her way to the kitchen. 'You women today want too much,' she said, over her shoulder.

Saloma stared at mother's retreating back and wondered how was it possible that she came from her loins.

Chapter 7

Saloma studied herself in her full-length mirror and liked what she saw. She looked casual yet modern and fun. Her white tank top left her arms and shoulders bare, and the short black skirt showed off her long, tawny-brown legs. Gathering her straight, raven-black hair into a ponytail, she donned gold hoop earrings and painted her full lips red. Humming a tune under her breath, she stepped out of her bedroom with her new short-strapped shoulder bag, snug beneath her left underarm. She still couldn't believe that Noah had actually called her. As much as she hated to admit it, she had been looking forward to seeing him again. 'And it wasn't a date,' she muttered to herself.

'Mummy, I'm about to leave for my lunch appointment,' she called out. The flat was quiet. Shrugging her shoulders, she slipped into a pair of low-heeled sandals, when the telephone rang. Her first impulse was to ignore it, it must be one of her mother's friends. Her hand wavered over the red cordless telephone as it rang a second time and a third. Finally, she decided to pick it up.

'Saloma. I'm glad I caught you! I was worried that you'd left!'

'Noah?'

'Yes!'

'Well, I was just about to. We're meeting at 12.30 right?' Saloma asked, puzzled.

'I'm so sorry, Saloma. I can't make it.'

'What do you mean? Did something happen?'

'It's my father's friend. He just met with an accident and I was told that he's in bad shape.'

'Oh, I'm sorry to hear that. Um . . . so, it was not your father? It was his friend?' Saloma asked.

Noah paused. She could hear him breathing. 'Yes, it was my father's friend. I know it sounds weird but I'm quite close to him. He spent a lot of time with me when I was growing up.'

'All right, of course. Take care.'

'I'll make it up to you. I promise. I'll call when I know better.'

Saloma put down the phone and tried to gather her thoughts.

'Sal? Are you leaving?' her mother asked.

'Um, oh no, Mummy. Change of plans.'

Her mother sat on a sofa and took a bite of her green apple. 'Was that him who called?'

Saloma shrug off her shoulder bag. 'Yes.'

'He can't make it?'

Saloma glanced at her mother and nodded her head.

'So, was he telling the truth? Or did he lie?'

'I'm not too sure, Mummy. He sounded sincere but his explanation did sound rather convenient,' Saloma answered, more to herself than to her mother.

'Men not so complicating,' her mother said as she reached for the remote and switched on the television.

It was a good ten days later, when she heard from Noah again. He was apologetic and insisted that they should meet. Despite her reservations, Saloma agreed to coffee on a Saturday afternoon instead of lunch or dinner. She was surprised when he suggested a new upbeat café that was known for their expensive beans and finger sandwiches.

He was early. She found him seated at a corner table with a panoramic view of the city. Dressed in a white shirt and black jeans, he stood up when she came to the table; his eyes, warm and contrite.

'Hi Saloma. Thanks for coming and for giving me a second chance. You look lovely.'

Saloma smiled and sat down opposite him. She crossed her arms, drawing attention to her bosom but Noah's eyes didn't stray from her face. It was the first time she saw him close-up. He was clean shaven but she could see where his beard would otherwise be growing as it was darker there. His eyes were surprisingly small and close under his light eyebrows, but his lips were full and generous. They would look good even curled in disdain.

'So, how is this *uncle* of yours?' Saloma asked, making herself comfortable in the high-backed chair.

Noah paused.

Saloma burst out laughing. 'Was that for dramatic effect?'

Noah looked puzzled. 'What?'

'You took some time to answer, and I just wondered?' Saloma said, tongue in cheek.

Noah looked genuinely confused and Saloma felt a slight discomfort.

'He died,' Noah blurted out.

Saloma sat upright and stared at him in disbelief. 'Your father's friend? Your *uncle*?'

Noah nodded.

'Is this a joke? You're kidding me, right?' Saloma asked, leaning forward.

Noah gave a startled look and Saloma shifted her feet under the table, surprised that he appeared genuinely upset.

She reached across the table and touched his hand lightly. 'I'm so sorry. What happened?'

Noah cleared his throat. 'He was involved in a car accident and passed away the same day. I was busy with the funeral preparations, and well, that was why I couldn't call you. I'm sorry about that.'

Saloma was at a loss. The pain in his eyes was too real.

'He was close to you, you said?'

'Um, yes. He was my father's friend since they were children. Childhood friends, I guess,' Noah elaborated, taking a quick sip of water.

Saloma waited for him to continue, waving the waitress away as she came to take their orders.

'So, he, Uncle Azad, was there for my birth and throughout my life actually. He was single. You know, I always wondered about that,' Noah said with a sudden frown. 'He was such a loving, kind man. Surely, a good woman would have seen those qualities? Anyway,' Noah continued with a shake of his head, 'he saw me as his son.' Noah smiled. 'My father used to joke that I saw him more as a father that he ever was and in some sense, I did.' Noah looked away and stared at the view below them. 'My father was a businessman and was often away. Don't get me wrong,' he hastened. 'My Mum and I didn't mind cos he worked so hard to give us a good life. Uncle Azad, on the other hand, was a teacher and was always just a phone call away. Even during the holidays, he preferred to stay in town, reading and writing. He was a poet, as well. Did I mention that?'

Saloma shook her head.

'Well, he was. I think he even compiled it into a book,' Noah said, trying to recall.

'So growing up, he was there at almost every single milestone in my life: birthdays, graduation, and even football games. You should have seen the number of his students who came to his funeral,' Noah said, eyes downcast.

Saloma nodded her head, though she wondered whether his uncle had been secretly in love with Noah's mother all those years.

'So, he was the one who inspired you to be a teacher?' Saloma asked instead.

'He certainly played a part but honestly, it came about by accident. My mother asked me to teach a couple of the kids in our neighbourhood during one of the school holidays. I was reluctant, but when she said the parents offered to pay good money, I could hardly refuse,' Noah said with a wink. 'Funny, how life is. If she hadn't, I wouldn't have known and maybe not even have met you on the train,' he said with a grin.

Saloma returned his smile and was relieved that they were on happier topics.

'So you believe in fate?' Saloma asked, curious.

Noah frowned. 'Well, I do think that there are some instances in our lives which are unavoidable or pre-determined. How about you?'

'At this moment, all I can think of is having a cup of coffee and maybe some of those delectable sandwiches,' Saloma said eyeing a waitress carrying a tray of food.

'How rude of me! Of course! I think I saw you waving the waitress away a couple of times,' Noah exclaimed.

'A couple of times? More like three or four,' Saloma said with a grin.

Noah hung his head in mock shame, and Saloma burst out laughing, glad that the mood had shifted.

The hours went by quickly, and Saloma was surprised at how easy it was to talk to him. It wasn't until the waitress placed the bill discreetly on the table that she realized that they were the last ones to leave. Noah took a quick glance at the bill and reached for his wallet, the smile still pinned on his face. Saloma excused herself and made her way to the restroom. Staring at her flushed face in the mirror, she reapplied her crimson lipstick and pulled her long hair to one side, exposing one gold hoop earring. Smiling at her reflection, Saloma made her way to the table and knew something was wrong the moment she saw Noah.

He was going through his wallet and taking out the contents on the table. The waitress was no longer at their table but Saloma saw her with two of her other colleagues, one of whom looked like the manager. They were talking in hushed tones and darting quick glances at Noah at the same time.

'Noah, is everything all right?' Saloma whispered, as she pulled out her chair to sit down.

Noah lifted his head, and Saloma drew back in alarm. His face was red, and his jaw worked furiously as he tried to come up with a response.

'Saloma, I'm so sorry. I'm such a fool.'

'What is it?'

'This has never happened to me before and trust me, I'm absolutely mortified,' he said, wiping his brow with a napkin.

Saloma's eyes travelled to his shirt and saw damp sweat patches under his arms. 'Tell me.'

'I forgot my credit card. I must have left it on my desk at home and . . . and I don't have enough cash on me.'

Saloma stared at him and tried to gather her thoughts. 'You sure know how to treat a girl like a real queen, Noah,' Saloma said, reaching for her credit card in her wallet and waving it to the waitress.

Noah shook his head and tucked his wallet back in his pocket.

'I will pay you back and will foot every single bill from now onwards.'

Saloma lifted an eyebrow as she signed the bill. 'Why, Noah, this is the perfect excuse not to meet me again. After all, you've got yourself a free meal.'

'Okay, I deserve that. This will haunt me forever, but trust me, I will make it up to you. How about dinner, next Saturday?' Noah asked, his face earnest. 'You choose the venue, and,' he said with deliberation, 'don't' bring your wallet.'

'Yes,' he repeated to the incredulity in her eyes. 'I will pick you up, bring you to the restaurant of your choice, entertain you with my wit, and *only* when you feel like it, I will send you home. Deal?' he finished, extending his right hand to her.

'Um . . . what do you mean by when I feel like going home?' Saloma asked, shaking his proffered hand.

'Just that! If you feel that the night is still young, I don't have to drive you home. We could catch a midnight movie or go for an evening stroll,' Noah said, leading her out of the restaurant just in time to hear the manager say to the waitress that served them: 'I don't know why Singaporean women love to date ang mo's. He got looks, manners but no *money*. What for!'

Saloma looked at Noah and burst out laughing. She stopped in her tracks and couldn't help a quick retort to the manager. 'It's okay, he has promised to pay for all my meal treats from now onwards,' Saloma said, looking at the waitress who was gawking at Noah.

'We have to go. I'm sorry again, and thanks,' Noah said to the waitress and steered Saloma to the lift.

True to his word, when they met the following weekend, Noah picked her up in his father's Audi, gifted her with a box of chocolates, and made no demur when she recommended a high-end French restaurant. He made a big fuss of checking her handbag and showed mock relief when he couldn't find her wallet. It was a delightful evening, and though Saloma was giddy with excitement, she didn't expect anything more from him. But every time she expected him to break a promise, to cancel an appointment, he showed up. He was punctual, gracious, witty, and almost impossible to distrust. He shared with her his life without any artifice while she painted a fuzzy image of her family; as if it was a footnote, something that was essential but out of sight.

One day, as they were watching the sun set at Sembawang jetty, he asked her about her father: 'When did he pass?'

Saloma studied a couple of anglers as they packed up their rods and their catch of fish and small crabs in pails of sea water. 'Do you know that you can see Johor from here?' she asked him instead.

'Yup, we're at the northern shore of Singapore after all. Do you know this very jetty we're standing on was built by the British in the 1940s but they abandoned it when the Japanese arrived. It was the Japanese who completed it,' Noah said, stamping on the wooden floors. 'Imagine if the floorboards could talk! The stories they could tell.'

Saloma chuckled. 'It would make a great movie but I'm sure these are not the original floorboards.'

'Let's imagine that they are. It's more fun. Do you know that you've a nice voice?'

'What do you mean?'

'Your voice. You have a lovely voice actually.'

'What are you talking about? I haven't been singing,' Saloma asked, perplexed.

'Oh, don't you realize that you hum all the time? There's tune that you always sing under your breath,' Noah said, with a laugh.

Saloma stared at Noah, and for a full second, her mind was a complete blank before she burst out laughing. 'I honestly didn't know that I was doing it! It's my father's favourite song. I grew up listening to it, and the happy tune stuck in my head, I guess.' Saloma sobered and whispered. 'My father, um, he died when I first started to work at the civil service, right after graduation. It was his liver. It gave way, after years of abuse,' Saloma said.

'Alcohol?' Noah asked, to which Saloma nodded.

'Is that why you don't drink?'

Saloma shrugged. 'I'm not too sure. Personally, I don't care for the taste,' she said with a face. 'And I also hate the feeling of not having control of my actions, my sensibilities, as they say,' she said, looking at Noah with a grin.

Noah nodded and threw a pebble into the water, creating ripples around it.

'That's so cool. I've always seen that in movies,' Saloma laughed. A gust of wind blew her straight black hair into her face, and Saloma paused to remove them.

'Why didn't you change jobs when your father passed? You strike me as someone who could do wonders in advertising, marketing, and even journalism. You have a way with people.'

'You think so?'

Noah looked down at her and smiled. 'Yes, I think so and so do *you*.'

'You're getting quite familiar with me.'

'I didn't mean any offence; it was a compliment actually,' Noah said, his face reddening.

Saloma touched his arm lightly.

'Gee, you're so easy to tease. Back to your question. Well, I did apply for those positions, and though I managed to get past their first or second interview, I never could get the job. I only knew the reason when one of the interviewers finally admitted the truth. They wanted someone who was well versed in Mandarin. Though I know a smattering of words,' Saloma said, gesticulating with her hands. 'I was not good enough to converse with clients or with the man on the street. It's a fact of life living here as a minority,' Saloma said with a slight lift of her shoulder. She glanced up at Noah. 'I tried broadcasting too but though they liked my overall looks,' Saloma said with air quotes. 'I still didn't get the job. One of the staff told me that it was my skin. I'm too dark, it seems, viewers prefer a light skinned person on television,' Saloma said with a laugh. 'It's strange that they came up with this belief,' Saloma said, in a sobered tone. 'If you watch or listen to BBC or CNN, they've a lot of journalists who have Indian and African heritage. I'm sure we can all agree that these news organizations are superior to our local media, but while they, our local media, seem happy to copy international broadcasters in many aspects, they stop when it comes to having darker skinned people on TV.'

Noah frowned and turned around so he could face her. 'That's so unfair. Surely, they're other places you could apply, one that needs a supreme command of the English language?'

'Thanks for the vote of confidence. I'm not angry. It's a fact I've lived with. And my father had told me long enough. I just need to find a way to succeed despite my background, to earn their respect and acceptance,' Saloma said, surprised by her own admission. 'It's a challenge being in my community. If we're part of the working class, it's cos we didn't work hard enough. It's our fault even though we make an honest living. I'm deemed a minah, if I'm uneducated but when I *am*, I still have to be careful, I have to un-Malay myself to suit the powers that be. I even had bosses and colleagues introduce me like this, "This is Saloma, she's Malay but don't worry she's very modern." What the hell does that mean? Malays are backward? Malays are old-fashioned? Yet, for all the so-called modern un-Malay qualities that I have, I still miss out on opportunities and promotions because at the end of the day, someone still decides based on your race. I can't get away from the colour of my skin,' Saloma said, looking out at the ocean. 'My father talks about the unfair 100 metre race where Malays have to run faster cos the other races are not at the starting line, they're further up. No one likes to acknowledge this here. But ironically, when they talk about successful Malays in Malaysia, people like to say, "Oh, Malays in Malaysia have all these advantages and support that's why they're more successful,"' Saloma said with a curl of her lip. 'Anyway,' she said with a playful smile on her lips, 'at the moment, I'm quite content at my current place of work. My colleagues are kind and my boss has promoted me several times. I'm fine.'

'How about you? Any dramas to share?' she said, tucking her hair behind her ear.

Noah pursed his lips and Saloma could see him thinking.

'Well, you know that I'm north Indian but my father was so light skinned that it was hard to tell. Maybe, if I looked traditionally Indian, I would be telling you a different story. So far, I haven't experienced what you have. Many of the Singaporeans are happy that I can lapse into proper Singlish when I want to and as a teacher, colour is not important, at least I hope so.'

'That's good. One day, I would like to,' Saloma paused. 'Never mind, it's getting dark, we better go,' she said, hugging her thin sweater around her body.

'Wait a minute. Finish your sentence. What would you like to do?'

'I would like to create my own jewellery line. I have tons of ideas! Be my own boss. Do something that's creative and imaginative.'

'So why don't you?'

'I'm saving but that's not enough. I need an investor, someone who's willing to bet on me.'

'*I'll* be more than happy to be your investor, if I have the money, of course!'

Saloma leaned her head against his arm. 'That's sweet of you, Noah. What about you? Are you happy where you are?'

Saloma felt him move and straightened her back.

'Let's find a place to sit,' Noah said, instead, steering her to the one of the park benches facing the sea. 'Comfortable?'

Saloma nodded her head, glad to give her feet a rest. She kicked off her sandals and sat cross-legged, facing his profile. 'So, tell me.'

Noah laughed and stretched out his legs, his arms behind his head. 'I love teaching, as you know,' he said, glancing at her sideways before shifting his gaze back to the grey waters, 'but I hate the politics.'

'In teaching?'

'Yup. It's like any other place,' Noah said to her incredulous look.

'I'm not interested in fighting for positions, I just want to teach. My principal said that I lack ambition,' Noah said. 'Maybe, he's right but if all that energy spent on pleasing the bosses and being politically correct, whatever that means, is channelled into teaching, into reaching out to *all* children and not just the brightest, I think, we can do a hell lot more!'

'So, what would you like to do?' Saloma asked, curious.

Noah stared out to the sea. 'I'd like to open up my own school,' he said as his voice was taken by a sudden gust of wind.

Saloma tied back her hair and buttoned up her sweater as she waited for Noah to continue.

'I mean not a school *school* but maybe a tuition agency or a centre where I can help them to do better, be better. Mind you, I'm not talking about those centres who pride themselves on helping the kids get As,' he said, curling his upper lip, 'but in maximizing their potential, whatever that maybe.'

'I like that business idea! What a pair we'll make: I have a jewellery line and you can have your dream teaching job!'

'We certainly need this big investor of yours,' Noah said with a burst of laughter.

'Actually, I don't think you need much, Noah, I mean to start your centre. Um . . . let's see,' Saloma said as she wriggled herself into a more comfortable position. 'You definitely need to rent a space and provide basic furniture, of course, advertise, though I don't think you need to do much as all the mums have your number,' Saloma said with a grin. 'Most important, I think is to get the centre certified by the Education Ministry, employ teachers trained by the Ministry, set up a curriculum that is acceptable and *you'd* have no problems with that,' Saloma said with excitement, 'and provide a safe environment. I think it's that easy cos you're already a teacher!'

'You make it sound doable, Sal! Well, if I ever get to pursue this venture, you can run it for me. I'll just be happy to teach.'

'It's a deal,' Saloma said, offering her hand, which he clasped tightly.

Saloma straightened her legs and winced.

'Pins and needles?'

'Yes, ouch. My legs have gone to sleep. It's getting better, no worries,' Saloma said to the look of concern in his eyes. She slipped into her shoes and looked around her. The lamp posts around the park had lit up and she could see groups of people cooking over charcoal grills at the designated barbeque pits. The smell of sausages and burnt chicken wafted in the air.

'What do you think about children?'

Saloma looked up. 'That's a random segue,' she teased. 'What about them?'

Noah laughed. 'Yes, that *was* an abrupt change of topic. So, do you? Want children, to be a mother?'

Saloma looked up into his questioning eyes and decided to be truthful. 'I like children; I do enjoy their company but . . . honestly, I don't see myself as a mother, as a parent. There are so many things that I want to do, to see, to accomplish by myself and with *you*,' she said, in a rush. She paused. 'I don't see children in the future, in *my* life, Noah,' Saloma whispered. She turned around and faced him squarely. 'Is that selfish of me?'

Noah brushed her face lightly with his fingertips. 'No,' he whispered. 'Not to me. I'm glad you're honest.' He cleared his throat. 'My father had always wanted a big family. He came from one but ironically, he wasn't close to any of his siblings. He kept saying that it was fun growing up with lots of children,' Noah said with a slight downturn of his mouth. 'Anyway, I remember him repeating that to us, to my Mum and I,' Noah hesitated. 'But I always felt that she wasn't so keen. It was only later, I realized that pregnancy was hard on her.' Noah jammed his hands into his sports jacket and continued, 'They tried and tried and in turn, my mother went through one harrowing miscarriage after another. I always wondered why she didn't tell him.' Noah turned to face the darkening sky and rubbed his arms. 'It was painful to watch her after each miscarriage. Her body just shut down. One day, my father had to call a doctor to our home as she was too exhausted to move. Before he left, the doctor told my father to accept reality and to just focus on me. Thankfully, my dad listened and things got better. She got better.' Noah took her hand and laced his fingers through hers. 'I realized then, that it's not up to *us*, us men, to decide. It's women like you who have to go through such monumental physical, mental, and emotional changes. It's *your* body. We have no right to ask and it's such a *big ask*, really.' Saloma leaned her head against his shoulder, brought their joined hands to her lips, and kissed his knuckles.

Saloma knew when he was going to propose. Before it even happened. The first clue was the weekend before the second anniversary of their first date when he came over to the house to see her mother. Saloma didn't know what was discussed but her mother was bright eyed when she mentioned Noah. It didn't take much prompting for her mother to reveal that Noah had asked for her blessings. On the day of their anniversary, he brought her on a nostalgic train ride, starting from Ang Mo Kio station where she had stolen his heart, he enthused, followed by a romantic dinner at the first French restaurant they went to in the early days of their relationship.

Saloma was ready. But she didn't expect her feelings to bubble over when he went down on one knee with the iconic forget-me-not-blue box in the palm of his hand. Conscious of the diners watching her reaction, Saloma nodded her head to which they burst into rapturous applause and whistles. Noah then slipped the 0.3 carat diamond onto her finger and though she wished it was far bigger, she smiled when she caught sight of their reflection in the mirror. His sandy blonde hair and the light hair that covered his forearm was a stark contrast to her warm caramel skin and dark chocolate tresses. She had come a long way she thought, but did she *really* deserve him?

Chapter 8

Saloma looked at the grandfather clock that had been in Noah's family for generations and tapped her burgundy fingernails on the dining table. Noah was taking longer than usual to dress up. Pushing back her chair, she walked barefooted to the house's only bathroom, and stood by the door. She could hear the water in the shower was still running. It was one of those things that she had discovered about Noah when they got married. He loved taking long hot showers and even though he took minutes to dress up, his time in the bathroom used to infuriate her in the early months of their marriage. Now, she hit the shower first. That way, she had the chance of having plenty of hot water for herself.

She caught sight of herself in the mirror over the wash basin and stopped in her tracks. She had kept her hair straight and long but the new golden-brown highlights made her skin brighter and she looked exotic, almost foreign. She smiled when she recalled her last ride in a taxi. It used to bother her growing up that when she took taxis, the Chinese drivers, without fail, would lapse into broken Malay rather than speak to her in English. She used to reply in her best clipped and precise English, hoping to distract them, but all she got was a confused, 'Huh?' followed by more pidgin Malay. But now, she loved it when they asked her where she was from, because she knew they no longer saw her as a second-class citizen. Does he think, I'm Italian, or Spanish she would ponder every now and again. She couldn't help herself and lied that she was Italian and suppressed a giggle with her hand.

Saloma headed to the living room and sat down on one of the vintage rattan chairs. The flower-patterned cushions felt threadbare under her. Muttering under her breath, she slid lower and stretched her legs out, crossing them on the coffee table. The rattan sofa set has been with Noah's family for more than thirty years, just like the rest of the furniture in the three-bedroom bungalow at Jalan Sendudok. They moved in with Noah's parents when they got married, and though Saloma was nervous, the elderly couple had treated her with respect and kindness. It was supposed to be a temporary measure until they could find something of their own but their untimely demise a year ago compelled Noah to stay longer. Saloma bided her time, and when she saw a new condominium development in the heart of the city that hadn't been constructed; she convinced Noah to accompany her to the launch. It had everything she wanted, especially the penthouse unit.

She studied the rows of empty vases of varying sizes and colours arranged on the shelf above the television set. They came from different parts of the world. Noah's mother was a collector and would painstakingly wipe each and every one of them every month. Once, Saloma had offered to fill them with flowers, but his mother had graciously declined, claiming that they didn't need flowers to make them beautiful. Saloma studied them from her slouched position and wondered not for the first time, whether they were of any value.

'Sal? I'm ready!' Noah called out, emerging into the living room with his hair slicked back and dressed in a short-sleeved white shirt with a pair of black trousers.

Saloma removed her legs from the coffee table and cocked her head to one side with curiosity. 'Are you sure about the shirt? Wouldn't a long sleeve shirt with a tie look better?'

Noah sat opposite Saloma on the three-seater sofa and looked down on himself. 'This is fine, it's not a formal meeting. Kok Liang and I go way back and he's such a cool guy. He wouldn't expect to me come in a business attire. I'm a teacher, not a businessman.'

The corners of Saloma's mouth curved up. 'Noah, you're a businessman, silly. In these three years, we have three centres, you have teachers working for you, not forgetting all the support staff.'

Noah reached for his shoes and leaned forward to tie them, crossing the laces and pulling them tight. 'Thanks to my parents. Even in death, they've contributed to my growth,' he said, his face flushed.

'Noah, are you regretting our decision to quit and this . . . this venture of ours?' Saloma asked.

Noah sat up. 'I'm sorry, I didn't mean to sound, I don't know . . . weird, I guess.' He expelled a breath and flapped his shirt. 'It's damn hot in here. I just had a shower and I need another one! Can you flip the switch for the fan?'

Saloma did as she was told and returned to her seat. She waited for Noah to continue. She knew it was pointless to rush him. She watched him lean back against the cushion as he studied the whirring blades above him, before he sat up and leaned towards her.

'Sal, they left me with a generous inheritance, and I don't want to make rash decisions. My father worked so hard to make his fortune. Growing up, we didn't have fancy holidays or expensive presents. My mother was all about good deals and stretching the dollar. I just want to . . . um . . . make the right decisions. Sal, I knew immediately, that it was a right move for me, for *us* to quit. It was a joy when we opened the first centre.' He looked deeply into her eyes. Saloma nodded and blinked. 'I was happy to teach full time and then, we opened the second and third. That was fine too as I still get to teach. But now, you're or *we're* thinking of making the centres island-wide, getting investors. That's huge,

Sal. And we haven't even started to work on your dream. Perhaps, we should discuss this jewellery business of yours and just take it slow with the centres.'

Saloma stood up and sat beside Noah on the three-seater. The thin, misshapen cushion slid under her. Swallowing an expletive, she pinned it under her butt and put her whole weight on it. 'Noah, it's too early to start my jewellery business. I'm still learning at LaSalle College. But your centres are doing so well. It's time to expand. Many parents have suggested we set up branches in neighbourhood towns. Closer to public housing, HDB. You haven't met Kok Liang in what, fifteen years, and just last week, he contacted you, out of the blue. I think the universe is telling us something.'

Noah sighed and leaned back. 'Sal, he didn't say that he wanted to invest in *our* business, he just said that he was looking for something creative to invest in cos that was what his father wanted. It's not his money, it's his family wealth.'

'So, what's wrong in just talking with him? Maybe, he can give us ideas, steer us in the right direction. He's the best person to talk to, Noah; his family has got a finger in every business there is.'

Noah paused, and for a moment, Saloma thought that he was going to refuse but then he stood up and said, 'All right then, let's go and pick his brains.'

However, the meeting was nothing like what Saloma expected. After the pleasantries, Kok Liang and his partner Simon advised them against expansion. They were told to celebrate their success and to stay put. Noah was relieved and was more than happy to end the meeting, but Saloma was stupefied.

On the way to the car, she realized that she had left her pair of sunglasses in Kok Liang's office. Kicking herself for the mistake, Saloma ran back to the elevator and made her way to his office, but it was empty when she opened the main door. They must be out for lunch, she thought as she hurried to Kok Liang's room, her footsteps swallowed by the thick rug. She raised her hand to knock on the door but stopped midway when she heard voices.

' . . . Noah and Cheryl,' Kok Liang said.

'What do you mean?'

Saloma leaned closer. It sounded like Simon, his partner.

'You know Cheryl, right? Cheryl Chew; her father is a big real estate developer and her mother owns many boutiques here and in Jakarta. Their wealth is off the charts. Anyway, their youngest daughter Cheryl is cool. She's nothing like the rich kids today. Hell, she is even better than me. Graduated with first class honours. She's got brains and beauty. And so down to earth, there's no airs about her. Well, I introduced her to Noah about six years ago.'

'I thought you haven't met him in fifteen years,' Saloma heard Simon ask.

'Oh, I didn't introduce them in person. I just sent him an email and asked whether he could meet up with her. That was how much I believed they were meant for each other. They went out on a couple of dates and she liked him. I know cos I asked her.'

Saloma couldn't hear Simon's reply.

'All right, she's not stunning, but she's poised, elegant, and well dressed. She ticks all the right boxes. She's a perfect foil for Noah. What a shame. Hell, he can do a whole lot better with *any* educated Chinese girl. With Saloma, well . . . Of course she looks great and speaks well. It's fine to have her as a girlfriend but as a *wife*? All I know is that my father can't trust a Eurasian and a Malay woman to set up educational centres all over the island. To be frank, I'm surprised they got this far. The Malays are not known for their educational qualifications, their business acumen. Sounds bad, yeah, but it's a fact, Simon. Let's not kid ourselves. You know, I heard from my Mum that some Malay girls have been known to use *charms* on men. Maybe, Saloma went to see one of those voodoo people and made Noah fall in love with her? What do they call it in Malay?'

'I think it's *bomoh*,' Simon said with a laugh. 'You're talking crazy now, bro!'

Saloma didn't bother to hear Kok Liang's reply as she dashed out of the room and sought the nearest washroom. Locking herself in one of the cubicles, she leaned over the cold porcelain and heaved the contents of her breakfast into the bowl.

It was nearly half an hour before she made her way back to the car. Noah was busy playing with the radio stations when she opened the passenger door. He looked up with a smile. 'Hey, I was wondering what took you so long? Kok Liang was jabbering again?' Noah said before he finally noticed her pale face. 'Sal, what's wrong?'

'I heard them talking,' Saloma said, looking straight ahead.

'What? Who? Kok Liang and Simon?'

Saloma nodded, not trusting herself to speak.

Noah unbuckled his seat belt and leaned towards her. 'So, tell me.'

Saloma cleared her throat. 'It was an excuse when he said that we should not expand, cos,' Saloma took a deep breath. 'Cos he didn't want to have anything to do with us, *with me*,' Saloma said, as she swallowed a sob. 'He said that Malays are not known for their education or have a business mind and that his father wouldn't trust us.'

'Wait what? Kok Liang said that? That two faced *bastard*! And all along, I thought he was happy for us. I'll tell him myself!' Noah said, as he reached for the door handle.

'No, wait, Noah. Please let me finish,' Saloma said clutching his wrist.

'I'm not going to change my mind. And he's wrong! You're good with numbers, you've a terrific business sense, and you run these centres like a superwoman. You even presented to him! I was just sitting there!'

'But he doesn't see that. All he understands are the stereotypes of my race.' Saloma dabbed her eyes. 'He also said that,' Saloma bit her lip. 'He said that it's impossible for you to fall for me,' Saloma heaved a sigh. 'So, I must have, have . . . seen a bomoh to make you fall in love with me, something only my race is known for.'

'That *bastard!* I've heard enough!' Noah said as he reached for the door.

'No, Noah, no! It will not solve anything. He'll just apologize and say he was sorry I overheard the conversation but . . . he would also say that it was . . . it was just his views and he's entitled to them.'

'Damn right! Those were his own twisted views!'

'We have to fight him, or people like him in a different way, don't you see?' Saloma said, as she leaned forward and looked deeply into Noah's eyes. 'We have to expand. If we remain as we are, people like him will say that we lack ambition, we're easily contented, lacking initiative. I can go on and on. We have to fight the fight. And that means moving up, making waves.'

'What do you mean? Make more than we already have? Who the bloody hell cares what other people think?'

'Noah, listen to me. Of course, we have enough as it is. We're comfortable and happy. But that's exactly what they expect of us. Don't you see,' Saloma pleaded. 'We have to prove them wrong! And the only way is to acquire more wealth. Money is more than just a medium of exchange. It buys us respect, social acceptance and well . . . it represents a key . . . a key to unlock this tight small circle of the very rich.'

'Sal, I really don't give two cents about them. We should live for *us*, do things that make *us* happy. That's all that matters. Who cares about the filthy rich? We've no idea where they get their wealth or whether they're good people, or hell, whether they deserve *my* respect!'

'Oh Noah, it's not that simple,' Saloma said with a bitter laugh. 'It's easy for you to say cos even though you're a mixed race, you look basically white. A white man is far superior than someone like me. Yes, yes,' Saloma said, with her hand up, 'I know what you're going to say. You did experience negative comments during your National Service in the army as you stuck out like a sore thumb. They called you ang mo or a potato eater but those comments were never as bad as what I've experienced and am still experiencing. *Noah*, I'm judged the moment I enter a room, without even having to say a word. I have to prove to them that I'm more than just my race, my skin. It's important to me. All I ask is your support, that's all. I'll do all the work, I'll find another investor, even if it kills me, yes, yes, I'm just kidding, and I'll prove to the Kok Liangs of the world that *I matter*, that I can make a difference.'

'But for how long?' Noah asked, a worried frown between his brows.

'Oh, sayang, as long as it takes,' Saloma said as she gathered him in her arms, wondering at the same time whether she should have mentioned Cheryl.

Chapter 9

The woman seated behind the reception desk smiled, as Saloma walked through the glass door; the name 'Skills Lab' emblazoned across it in bold black letters. Saloma returned the gesture and took a swift appraisal of the lobby before turning to face the receptionist.

'Any calls for me, Winnie?'

The bare-faced woman with a tight ponytail swivelled to face Saloma and shook her head. 'Um . . . Nothing for you, Mrs Salem, just the usual enquiries from parents. We're fully booked this semester, but some of the parents begged me to call them if there was any cancellation.'

'Okay, that's good. Is Mr Salem still teaching?'

'Um . . . yes, he's teaching the whole day as one of the teachers is on medical leave.'

Saloma frowned, 'Which teacher?'

'Saloma! So nice to see you!'

Saloma whirled around and came face to face with a tall, tanned woman in workout attire.

'Susan, how are you?' Saloma said in surprise. 'Just finished a workout?'

Susan laughed, a loud boisterous laugh that filled the room. '*Ya lor*. Just finished my spin class. Very tough but so fun. Haven't seen you lately.'

Saloma winced at her use of Singlish. 'I could have been at the other centres so I guess we must have missed each other.'

'Aiyah, I come here every day. Today, I brought my youngest boy.' She looked around her and hollered at a young boy standing by the water cooler: 'David, come and say hello to Aunty Saloma.'

Saloma watched bemused as the bespectacled boy in shorts, t-shirt, and flip flops, walked towards her, his eyes downcast.

She knelt down and faced him. 'How are you David? Have you taken your lunch?'

'That boy is a fussy eater. He had a snack in the car,' Susan piped out.

Saloma looked up. 'He looks tired, Susan. We've snacks in the classroom. Fruits, nuts, and some sandwiches. I'll let Winnie know before he goes into class.'

'That's why your centre is *so good*! You and Noah are always concerned about the *chilren*. When they're tired in class, Noah asked them to do jumping jacks or some stretching. Exercise is *sooo* important. Keep them alert. Give them new brain cells. That's why I'm always moving. Spin class. Cycling. Aerobics.' Susan giggled. 'And some dancing too.' She moved her hips and hummed the latest pop song.

Saloma watched her belly jiggle under the tight top and hid a smile.

'Come and join me, Saloma!' she exclaimed, reaching for her hand.

'It's all right, Susan. I'm not much of a dancer,' Saloma said, backing away.

'Aiyah, you're so shy. You're so slim, tall and pretty. Even if you make a mistake, you'll still look good,' Susan said, running her eyes over Saloma's slim-fitted trousers and long-sleeved silk blouse.

'But once you've *chilren* it's hard to reduce. Look at me,' Susan exclaimed, grabbing the folds of her belly. 'After three *chilren*, this is very hard to reduce. I exercise five times, sometimes six times *leh*, but still it's there. A reminder.' she giggled. 'Hey, you and Noah *sooo* good looking, when are you making babies' she asked, with a wink. 'You cannot wait too long. We women have expiry date,' she said with a chuckle. 'Marriage must have *chilren*, if not, why marry? Also *chilren* are good for men. Keep them busy from other things,' she guffawed with another wink. 'You know what I mean, right. I can imagine your son or daughter,' she said, closing her eyes. 'Have your hair but Noah's eyes. He's really like ang mo. With your hair and his features, wah, super pretty or handsome,' she said, with a shake of her head.

'Speaking of which, where's your son? He was standing just next to you a moment ago?' Saloma asked, her lips tightening.

'He's there at the water cooler,' Susan said, with a shrug. 'Actually, David's class is tomorrow but when one of the mums told me on Facebook that Noah will teach his class today, I rushed to change his class schedule. Can't miss the chance. My boy here didn't do so well for his test. Noah can help.'

'David can just wait outside the classroom. There are chairs for him to sit. Winnie can help,' Saloma said, catching Winnie's eye.

'That's a good idea. I'll be back to pick you up when you're done, David!' Susan shouted as she pulled the main door wide open. 'Good to see you, Saloma!' she said as the door closed behind her.

Saloma expelled the breath she'd been holding.

'She's like that with everyone, Mrs Salem.'

Saloma turned to the sound of the voice and found Winnie looking at her.

'Um . . . what?'

Winnie stood up and leaned across the reception desk. 'Susan, is like that with everyone. She's tactless but she's not mean.'

'Is that right,' Saloma said, her eyebrows raised. 'I'll be at the accounts section,' she said, heading to the office, relieved to focus on something important.

She stayed at the office for three hours, longer than she intended. When she entered the front lobby, Winnie was busy attending to walk-ins, and she slipped out unnoticed. In the car, Saloma fiddled with the radio stations, hoping to hear a piece of music that would relax her. A thin layer of sweat, ran down her back at the thought of paying a visit to her mother. She had delayed it for far too long, the last time she saw her was nearly two months ago. Saloma gave up on the radio and hummed under her breath, as she started the car.

It was harder than she had envisaged, her mother barely moved her lips when she opened her front door. The television was switched on and there was a cup of tea next to the leather armchair. Her mother retreated back to her chair and her soap opera while Saloma stood by the door. Swallowing a sigh, Saloma took a seat next to her and fixed her eyes on the screen but saw nothing.

'She cannot have children,' her mother finally said, barely lifting her eyes from the television.

'What? I don't understand, who is this she?' Saloma asked, alarmed.

Her mother looked at her sideways, annoyed. 'This drama. Eh . . . you not watching? This woman in blue dress cannot have children so her husband leave her.'

'What kind of drama is this? Seriously, all these Malay soaps are mind numbing,' Saloma said, relieved that her mother was speaking to her. Leaning against the back rest, she closed her eyes.

'Open your eyes! You see that woman in blue dress?' her mother repeated, wagging her slightly bent forefinger at the television. 'That one,' she stressed.

Saloma opened one eye and obeyed her mother. 'What about her?'

'I say she cannot have children. Her husband leave her. I tell you three times now,' she said, shifting in her seat.

'He left her because of that. Perhaps, it's his fault. Did they see a doctor?'

'See a doctor? What for? Of course, her fault,' her mother retorted, frowning.

'Mummy, it's not always the women's fault. Sometimes, it's the men too. This drama is ridiculous. The director and writers should be sacked.'

'How to force men to see doctor for this? I cannot make your father to see doctor for his coughing, you think he go because of no baby?'

Saloma burst out laughing. Her mother was right. She couldn't imagine her late father sitting in the doctor's office talking about conception. 'But that was your generation, it's different today.'

'When it comes to making baby, all men the same. You think your Noah will go?' her mother challenged, her eyes narrowing.

'If that situation arises, of course he will. But as we don't want children, the subject doesn't arise,' Saloma said, standing up and making her way to the kitchen. 'I'm getting a drink, Mummy, would you like one?'

'I have my tea here,' her mother replied, a little irritable. As Saloma came back from the kitchen, her mother continued, 'Actually, I think and think but now I going to ask,' she said, her voice rising.

'What is it? Since when do you need permission, Mummy?' Saloma said, taking a sip of her water as she sat down.

Her mother snorted and looked at the screen. 'Why you marry if you don't want children?'

Saloma sighed. 'Why is everybody asking me this question? Is the world going to collapse just because Noah and I don't want kids?'

'I'm your mother. Not those busy bodies at your centre asking you. So why?'

'Mummy, I don't have a different set of explanations for you and another one for the rest of the world. It's not that complex,' Saloma said, staring at the screen. 'Noah and I want to focus on our careers and on us. Not all of us need children to complete our lives. What's wrong with that?'

'Look at me, Sal,' her mother demanded, as she swivelled the armchair so that she was facing Saloma.

'Oh all right, I'm listening,' Saloma said.

'Sal, our *one* important job,' her mother stressed, 'is make babies, be a mother.'

'That's why God give us this and this,' her mother said, grabbing her own breasts and groin.

Saloma groaned. 'Mummy, please, stop this.'

'You listen,' she said, wagging her finger. 'Children make marriage better. Men learn to take care of family. He make mistakes. But always go back to wife and children. Always. Listen to me.'

'Things are different now, Mummy. We have our own baby, our business,' Saloma said with a chuckle.

'This funny to you, is it? All you think is money, money, money. When is enough?'

Saloma paused. Staring at the rings on her finger, she said: 'Money is important because with it, comes respect and well . . . acceptance from society. That's how it works.'

'Hmm. You think money can change skin colour? Culture? You stupid, Sal. You chase wrong thing. We never can win. Be a mother. Wife. Noah will find you boring, one day. You never enough. We,' her mother patted her chest, 'we cannot be enough.'

'Why didn't you have more children then?' Saloma countered. For a full minute, Saloma thought that she had overstepped her boundaries. Her mother's slight figure was motionless; like a thing made of bronze.

'None of your business,' her mother finally spoke, her voice so low, that Saloma had to lean closer to hear her.

Saloma bit her lip. 'That's not fair, Mummy. You asked me so many personal questions and yet you hardly share with me your life,' Saloma said with a slight tremor in her voice.

Her mother lifted her chin. 'I'm your mother. I made you. I can ask anything.'

'But isn't it as a mother that you're supposed to steer me, guide me? How can you expect to accomplish that if you hide your life from me?'

'How clever you answer. Use big words. You think I stupid old cow?'

Saloma hid a sigh. This was getting nowhere. She sat closer to her mother and took her hand in both of hers. 'Mummy, you talked about marriage, children. What's so wrong in sharing with me *your* life, as a wife and as a mother?'

Her mother snatched her hands away and turned her chair to face the television. With her eyes fixed on the screen, she said: 'Nothing to tell. You and Noah must have children. Married three years now. You see this show? Husband left her because no children. So she ask him to stay and marry her sister. Sister become second wife.'

Saloma couldn't believe her ears. 'You're comparing my life with this . . . this nonsensical drama?'

'All dramas come from true stories. This not in writer's head,' her mother said, curling her lips.

'Well, then she's stupid. She should divorce him and get a better life,' Saloma declared.

'She not stupid. Actually, she clever. She control husband life now. She pick sister, so she control sister. Husband get baby and she get husband.'

'But . . . this means he gets to sleep with two women! How can that be right?' Saloma stammered.

Her mother turned around and spoke with pure honesty, 'One never enough, Sal. Never enough.'

Chapter 10

Saloma kicked off her shoes and hurried into the bedroom. 'Noah, I'm home! I've got great news! Noah?' Saloma studied the empty room and headed to the bathroom. The door was wide open but it was just as empty. 'Noah?' She walked to the kitchen and opened the back door that led to the yard. She slipped on a pair of slippers and found him stretching his hamstrings on the bench, his back facing her.

'Noah, there you are! Didn't you hear me?' She patted his back and he jumped back in alarm. 'Hey, it's only me. What's wrong with you?' Saloma asked, with a laugh.

'Gosh, I'm sorry!' Noah exclaimed, taking off his earbuds from his ears.

'Noah, one day, you're seriously going to damage your eardrums, listening to such excessive loud music!'

'I'm sorry,' Noah said, wiping his brow and chest with a towel.

'How was your run?'

'It was a relief! I've been teaching non-stop and it felt good just to move my body. All okay at the centres? The accounts?'

'Yes and yes! And speaking of the centres, I've good news to share. Why don't you take a shower first and I'll give you all the details later?'

Noah raised his eyebrows and sat down on the bench, his arms hanging between his legs. 'Tell me now. You've piqued my interest.'

Saloma hitched up her jeans and sat cross-legged facing him. 'You remember, Anne, right? I used to work with her at the Media Development Authority,' Saloma elaborated to which Noah nodded in acknowledgement. 'Well, I bumped into her several months back at some event and she introduced me to this formidable lady, Madam Khoo. Anyway, this lady, Madam Khoo, she's a businesswoman slash philanthropist amongst other things, and she showed interest when I mentioned to her about our tuition centres. I didn't think much of it back then cos I thought she was just being polite. But this morning, she called me and said that she heard we wanted to expand and Noah . . . guess what? She wants to invest in *us*. She believes in your innovative teaching skills. And . . . *and*,' Saloma exclaimed, 'She said she *loved* the brooch I made for Anne and said my idea of reinventing old vintage jewellery into something new and modern is captivating! Her daughter, Cass, runs their jewellery business and she said she'll hook us up! This is unbelievable!'

Noah stared at Saloma and rubbed his jaw. 'Oh, I didn't expect you to find an investor so fast,' he said, slowly. 'By the way, I have your sunglasses. Kok Liang had someone to send it to one of the centres.'

Saloma waved her hands. 'Sure. But isn't this just fantastic! One door closes and another one just opens. Madam Khoo was so positive and encouraging. She wants to meet us and talk about the details. She said your name has been circulating. Imagine that, Noah! I can meet her if you're busy. You know, how I love to talk shop!' Saloma said with a grin, her eyes bright.

Noah looked up and studied the mango tree, next to the fence. Saloma waited with her fists clenched, feeling her nails biting into her palms. She took a deep breath and tried to quell the excitement coursing through her.

Noah finally spoke, turning sideways to catch her eye. 'Sal, I've been thinking, I understood what you said earlier about proving them wrong, to fight the stereotypes they have of your race but . . . but we should do what's right for us. We have more than enough today, enough to start your jewellery line on a small scale, why do we need to expand? At this moment, we hardly have time together let alone to pursue our big plans of seeing the world.'

Saloma grabbed his hand and placed it on her cheek. 'We *are* planning for our future. This is an opportunity we cannot miss. We have to try it, Noah, if not we'll always wonder.'

Noah pulled his hand away and leaned against the backrest of the bench, his legs stretched out before him. 'I won't wonder, Sal, so it must be you. This island-wide expansion . . . Oh, Sal, let's just forget about that.' He turned to face her, grabbing both of her hands in his. 'Let's just get away. Go for a holiday. And when we're back, let me handle the centres, there's no need for you to oversee the accounts. What do you say?'

Saloma paused, not understanding. 'You mean, you want me to stay at home? What about my course? My dream?'

Noah cleared his throat. 'I didn't mean that you throw away your goals, or your dream as you said. I meant to just take a break from all this . . . this talk of business. I will cut back too.'

Saloma rubbed her eyebrows and bit the side of her lip. 'I see.' She cleared her throat. 'Um . . . how about if I just meet Madam Khoo and hear what she has to say? We can reach out to more kids if we expand, Noah . . . and with an investor, we can even subsidize kids who come from broken families or those who have financial difficulties. At the moment, our centres are in the city, accessible to kids from rich families but if we go to the heartlands . . . we can do more.'

Noah wiped his brow and stood up, his back ramrod straight. He looked aloof from where she sat, his stubbled jaw clenched and his face distant. He threw the towel over his shoulder and nodded. 'Okay,' he said, before loping off to the house.

Saloma stared at his retreating back and twisted her wedding rings absently. He'll come around, she thought. He always does.

The next six months were a blur of activity. A team of consultants swooped in, and before Saloma knew it, Madam Khoo's team had put before her a map of their proposed island-wide centres, with a brand-new corporate identity. Words such as uniformity, common processes, organizational charts, and constant messaging in marketing campaigns became her new vernacular. Noah showed little interest until they approached him to create a teaching methodology. He was happy to comply and to train future teaching staff but didn't share their enthusiasm in crafting a special programme to help a select group of potential students in achieving full marks.

'It's a niche programme, Noah,' Saloma explained. 'It's only for kids who have the potential and it's only for Maths. There will be no pressure. I know how you hate parents who force their kids to get As but this is different. Specialists will train our teachers to identify these kids and steer them in the right way. It'll be a small unit and if it succeeds, we'll expand,' Saloma pleaded.

Noah had remained quiet and though he nodded his head, Saloma wasn't so sure he was convinced. He declined to be interviewed by the press, but caved in when one of his former students, majoring in journalism, requested for an interview. It was a fun piece and was published in the campus publication but the local news agencies got wind of it and it was reprinted.

'You look so youthful and fun, Noah,' Saloma had said, gazing at his photo that accompanied the article. Noah had shrugged it off but Saloma knew that it was the right form of publicity that the business needed. She wasn't wrong, the following day, the three centres were swamped with calls, with parents eager to know the opening date of the new centres.

Chapter 11

It was nine on a Monday morning, almost a year into the expansion, when Saloma strode into the training room, fully aware that she was two hours early for her appointment with Cass. Cass Khoo, *the* jewellery mogul. How many times had she repeated that name over and over in her head. Saloma did a little jig. Things were slowly but surely coming into place. She reached for her smart phone and retrieved the simple email Cass sent her during the weekend, requesting for a meeting at eleven in the morning at the training centre. Saloma smiled and hummed a tune under her breath. Slipping the phone into her bag, she wished she could have discussed the meeting with Noah, but he had been quiet lately, more so than ever. She knew he was a little overwhelmed by all the changes. It is only a matter of time before he gets used to it, she mused.

Saloma took a step back when Cass Khoo eventually walked into the room. She looked nothing like her photographs. Her hair was pulled back in a tight ponytail, to expose a clipped short undercut and a row of small diamond studs and hoops that went all the way up her left ear and conch. Her petite, almost androgenous, body was covered in a standard yoga outfit of a loose tank top over a sports bra and a pair of black leggings. Her face was unblemished and she looked younger that her forty years of age. Insanely private about her personal life, Saloma could only gather from news clippings that she was the youngest child and only daughter of Madam Khoo and Clement Lim and had caused quite a stir when she took her mother's maiden name when she turned twenty-one.

Her company website described her as a rare jeweller with integrity in business. She attended the prestigious Goldsmiths, University of London, to study jewellery design but left midway to work as an intern at Tiffany and then later to the Gemological Institute of America where she learned the foundation of jewellery business. She took over the family jewellery business when she returned and pulled it back from the edge with her staunch views on ethically sourced stones and recycled gold. 'Jewellery,' she was quoted in her company profile, 'should be beautiful and ethically sourced.' Saloma was ecstatic, upon reading it—it meant that her vision to repurpose old jewellery could work hand in glove with Cass's business strategy.

Saloma pinned a warm smile on her face and extended her hand, conscious that she was overdressed for the meeting.

'Saloma, thank you for meeting me here. It's so much better than meeting at a café or a restaurant,' Cass said, looking around the room with interest. Her voice was soft and without an accent except when it came to the treatment of vowels; her voice took on a clipped British intonation. Saloma remembered that she lived in London for the best part of her growing up years.

'The pleasure is all mine. This is our training room and it's equipped with the state-of-the-art audio and visual technology. Your mother's team has done wonders. We have officially completed our island-wide expansion. This is our headquarters, hence our training centre is here,' Saloma said, looking around her with pleasure. 'Please take a seat,' Saloma said, ushering her to the lounge area. 'This is where we collaborate, exchange ideas, and also unwind,' Saloma said, taking a seat on the two-seater sofa, glad that they were now both at eye level.

Cass took the opposite armchair and reached for her water bottle in her black sports bag.

'Let me get you a drink, would you prefer still or sparkling water,' Saloma said, standing up but Cass motioned her to sit down as she emptied the bottle in one long gulp.

'So,' Cass said, as she screwed the lid back on her water bottle, 'I saw your work and I must say that I'm intrigued. Would you be able to come up with more designs?'

'Yes, of course!' Saloma said, a little quickly.

'I know many women have inherited jewellery that they have no interest in wearing, but with this method of remodelling, we can have sustainable jewellery.'

Saloma nodded her head in agreement.

'This idea is not new of course,' Cass elaborated. 'I've seen it being done in the West but here in Singapore, we have a trove of traditional jewellery from our own multicultural people. I love how you modernized your mother's fifty-year-old *kerongsang kebaya* into several modern brooches. In fact, I noticed from the photos and drawings that you retained some aspects of the original design and incorporated them in the new brooches. It would have been so much easier to melt the gold and make something completely new.'

Saloma beamed. 'I'm so glad that you noticed. Many craftsmen I met told me to do the exact same thing. In fact,' Saloma paused.

Cass raised an eyebrow.

Saloma wavered and took a deep breath. 'In fact, they said that my vintage pieces, especially my mum's, are so archaic and old-fashioned that it's best just to melt them.'

'That's such a waste,' Cass replied with a frown. 'Just your mother's?'

'Yes. I did have some jade pieces that I got from some close friends and they seemed more motivated to do them. Perhaps, they were more familiar with jade than my mother's Malay vintage pieces,' Saloma said with a wry smile. 'Anyway, I decided to refashion them on my own.'

'You're right. Obviously, they're more familiar with jade. What a shame. Anyway, I like that you honour the original design and make it into new. That requires ingenuity and creativity and of course, hard work,' Cass said with a smile.

'Um, you're too kind,' Saloma said, hoping her eagerness didn't show.

'I was wondering whether you could help me,' Cass said, her eyes never leaving Saloma's face. 'Eileen, a good friend of mine, is exhibiting her collection next weekend and the person who's doing her jewellery bailed out at the last minute. She needs a few bold pieces. Her whole collection is based on recycled materials so you're the right person I'm talking to. Would you be interested?'

'Next weekend? Um, that's quite tight but I can't resist a challenge,' Saloma said with a laugh. 'Perhaps, you could give me her contact number and I can proceed from there?'

'That's perfect,' Cass said, standing up. 'I'll send her a text and both of you can work out the details.'

'Thank you,' Saloma said, walking her to the door.

'I don't mean to cut this short,' Cass said, as she held the door handle. 'But I have to rush for my aerial yoga class, and I think, I may just get there in time,' she said, glancing at the sports watch on her wrist. 'Have a good day,' she said as she slipped through the door with a smile.

Saloma stared at the closed door for a few seconds and burst out laughing, moving her body in a little dance of celebration. She may have a chance to work with Cass if she played her cards right. All she needed to do was to produce a few stunning pieces. She studied her schedule and knew she had to clear her calendar till the start of the show.

The next couple of days were a whirlwind of activity. She met Eileen and liked her immediately. She was down to earth, funny, and talented despite her wealth and upbringing. They studied Saloma's vintage pieces and came up with a plan. The work cut out for Saloma was challenging but it helped that Noah was called away for army reserve training in Thailand, giving her the time she needed to focus and create.

On the day of the event, Saloma made sure to arrive early. It was held at a private residence of one of the developers Saloma had only read about. The mansion came complete with a lush garden decorated for the event with foliage, fauna, a water fountain, and flowers of every imaginable colour. A natural sandy pathway was used as a catwalk and the two rows of white chairs flanking it meant that only a select few were invited. For a moment, Saloma stood transfixed, trying to absorb every single luxurious detail. She caught sight of Eileen and waved at her. Eileen detached herself from the crowd and approached Saloma with a warm smile. They went to work immediately, pairing the jewellery with each outfit, and Saloma was delighted that her pieces were a perfect match with Eileen's collection.

The show was a success and Saloma joined the guests for snacks and drinks in the courtyard. Some of the guests looked familiar, she noticed a few editors of the local magazines, models, and several actresses from the local Chinese dramas. How she wished Noah was beside her.

'Hi Saloma, I *lurve* your jewellery. They were a perfect match with Eileen's collection. Did you study at Goldsmiths with Eileen and Cass?' a voice piped out.

Saloma turned to the sound of the voice and found a woman looking up at her. Her face, untouched by the sun, was pasty and her eyes, lined with black eyeliner looked unnaturally bigger than her small mouth.

'That's kind of you, thank you,' Saloma said, taking a sip of her drink. 'No, I met Cass and Eileen only recently.'

'Oh, so where did you learn jewellery design? Parsons in New York?'

Saloma gripped her cold drink in her hand and wished she could place it against her hot cheeks.

'Um, I graduated with honours at the local university but jewellery design has always been my passion. I took it up later in life and learned more about it at LaSalle,' Saloma said with a smile, glad that Cass had decided to join them, looking different in a white shirt and a pair of linen trousers.

'You don't need a degree to be a designer, Irene,' Cass said. 'Look at me, I didn't even finish my degree.'

Saloma smiled at Cass with relief.

'Cass! Lovely to see you,' Irene exclaimed, giving her a hug. 'How's your mother? I've been trying to meet her for lunch but she's always so busy! Let me look at you,' Irene said, holding Cass at arm's length and studying her outfit. 'You look wonderful, as always!'

'Thanks Irene,' Cass said, accepting a glass of champagne from a waiter. 'Mummy works non-stop. She loves her work. Just like Saloma. She's not only a jeweller but she also owns Skills Lab, *the* centre that saves kids and parents.'

'Ah, I remember reading about it. Didn't your mother have a hand in it?' Irene asked, popping a tart into her mouth.

'Mummy knows a good investment when she sees one.'

'That I know for sure,' Irene said. 'I've been telling Saloma that I love her designs.'

'That's exactly why I'm here, to tell her that! *Gorge* pieces, Saloma,' Cass said, looking at Saloma with a wide smile.

Saloma swallowed a lump and smiled, hoping her emotions wouldn't bubble over.

'I understand that those brooches came from your mother's kerongsang. Does that mean that you specialize in Malay jewellery?'

'Oh no, I remodel all types of jewellery. It just so happens that those belonged to my mother. If you have some family heirlooms that you'd like to refashion, let me know. I'll retain some of the original design so that it's not completely lost. It could be a great gift for your daughters or daughters-in law,' Saloma said with a smile. 'Especially, if they're looking for "something borrowed, something new."'

'That's an excellent idea. Do you have a studio, an atelier? I would like to see the rest of your work,' Irene declared.

'What did I hear? You have an atelier?' a smooth voice called out.

Saloma turned and came face to face with a tall pale woman, her eyes with their long curling lashes were looking straight at Saloma.

'Hi, I'm Denise and you must be Saloma,' she said, sipping from the flute glass.

'Nice to meet you. I'm just starting out, so I don't have a boutique at the moment,' Saloma replied with a smile.

'I think an atelier is something we can certainly discuss,' Cass said.

Saloma turned to face her with a look of incredulity in her eyes.

'Isn't it wonderful to have Cass in your life,' Denise purred, giving Saloma a discreet run down. 'So, tell me about yourself. I heard you went to one of the local universities. What year was it? You're too young to enjoy the free education our government gave out to the Malays in the 80's. So, it must have been the 90's?' Denise asked.

'Free education? Since when did we have free education?' Irene spluttered.

'In the 80's the government gave free education to the Malay community. While the rest of our parents paid taxes, they enjoyed a free ride. A pity, many of them didn't take up the generous opportunity,' Denise said.

Saloma stiffened. She opened her mouth to reply but her tongue felt heavy.

'No politics at a fashion show, Denise,' Cass admonished.

'Of course. Silly of me. Politics can be such a bore,' Denise said, moving away.

'Irene, I'm taking Saloma away. You've been monopolizing her too long, I need to introduce her to the rest of the party,' Cass said, with a wink, leading Saloma out of the courtyard.

'Thanks Cass,' Saloma whispered, wiping her sweaty palms with a napkin.

Cass gave her the same familiar grin, and Saloma couldn't help but smile in return.

'We need to spread your name and make a few ripples in the water, so to speak. What you've done today is incredible. I can't imagine what you can do with twice the time and one or two craftsmen to assist you,' Cass said, waving to some familiar faces.

'Craftsmen?' Saloma asked, unsure if she'd misheard her.

'Yes, my craftsmen in Bali, Lombok, and Bangkok.'

'And why do we need their help?'

'You've talent, Saloma. I can see that and I'd like to work with you,' Cass said, looking at Saloma. 'Do you have time? I know you have a tuition empire to oversee,' Cass said with a laugh. 'But can you take some time off and accompany me to Bali?'

'I would love to,' Saloma said, beaming at Cass, her eyes bright.

'Great. That's settled then. Let us now do the rounds,' Cass said, leading Saloma by the elbow.

True to her word, Cass introduced Saloma to all the guests. She tried to make a mental note of all their names and place of work. They appeared interested, and some of them even knew about Skills Lab, but Saloma knew they were just being polite. One or two even assumed she had a jewellery store at Malay Village on the sheer basis of her race.

It's going to be an uphill battle, she thought as she drove home, but with Cass's influence, she could make it work. No way was she going to give up, she thought as she sped, humming a familiar tune under her breath.

Chapter 12

It was ten in the morning and the private beach was slowly filling up. Saloma walked along the shore, curling her toes in the sand and feeling the warm water lapping at her feet. She tasted the salt air on her lips and laughed when a sudden gust of wind blew in, jamming her-wide brimmed hat down on her head. Her thin, white kaftan billowed out around her, like a sail. A waiter caught her eye and pointed to a lounge chair under a wide umbrella, where palm trees spread cool shadows out over the sand. Saloma nodded and made her way, all too aware that she was the only one covered from head to toe.

Humming under her breath, she made herself comfortable and watched with amusement as a toddler with his young parents laughed when the waves rolled in and washed away his sandcastle. The child, a boy no more than two years old, picked up his plastic mould and promptly built another one, only to shriek again when the tide came in and swept it away. His parents acted surprised every time it happened, making him laugh even more. Saloma smiled and closed her eyes. Even in the shade, she could feel the heat through her eyelids. It had been a long time since she felt renewed and energized. She was excited when Cass first suggested the ten-day trip but as the trip got nearer and she had more time to think about it, she began to worry about the prospect of being apart from Noah. She had never been away from him and the business for that length of time, but Cass was insistent. She wanted Saloma to immerse herself in jewellery design and to learn as much as possible. That meant meeting her craftsmen, studying the handcrafted jewellery that Bali was known for, and interacting with the artisans. It was almost like a full-time job as they were out in the morning and back in the evening, almost always using Cass's only mode of transport: her scooter. It was the first time for Saloma to discover the narrow streets in Kuta and Seminyak on the back of a motorcycle. Cass was right; it was the best way to appreciate the island. The locals stopped and smiled when they saw Cass kicking the bike to life with precision, while Saloma struggled to straddle the seat behind her. It was a comical sight: a long-legged woman hunched over a woman half her size. But whatever awkwardness she felt melted away as Cass didn't seem to mind the attention, and sometimes, she even encouraged it with a big wave and a cheeky smile.

Cass spared no expense when it came to accommodation. She chose a resort perched on the coast of Bali, known for its beautiful sunsets. Their private villa was a modern remake of the traditional Balinese courtyard house facing the ocean and in the evenings, they were within walking distance of the famous seafood restaurants at Jimbaran Bay. However, Saloma recognized that despite Cass's easy-going nature, she kept Saloma at a friendly distance and steered clear of personal topics.

'Hey, why are you hiding away in this corner? Come on, get up and let's hit the waves.'

Saloma opened her eyes and sat up, wiping her arms. 'Cass, stop it! You're dripping all over me!'

'Oh, sorry, is this mine?' Cass asked, reaching for a towel without waiting for an answer.

Saloma looked up and watched as Cass dried her hair and wiped her body. Over a few days, she had developed a golden tan which complemented her two-piece gold swimsuit. Saloma was surprised at how comfortable Cass was with her body, sunbathing nude on the deck of their villa with such natural ease. Her body was strong and firm; her small high breasts and boyish hips gave her an athletic appeal. Sports came easily to her, and Saloma had seen her balancing on the paddle boat, kayaking, and playing softball on the beach with the other guests. She was by far the most intriguing person Saloma had ever met.

'You've stuck yourself in the shade, covered yourself from head toe, and yet you're on the beach,' Cass said, a wide smile on her face.

Saloma burst out laughing and took off her sunglasses. 'Well, unlike you, I tan so easily. This is the only way I get to enjoy the sun and sea without turning black like the bottom of the well.'

'What are you talking about? You've got beautiful skin. People in the West would pay good money to have that colour. Are you fishing for compliments?'

'What?' Saloma asked, startled.

Cass looked at her briefly and put down her towel. 'Um, I guess you're not. Enjoy the sun, you've worked hard these five days. Go and have a dip in the water. It's nice and warm.'

'I'm happy here,' Saloma said stretching out her legs.

'Suit yourself,' Cass said as she sat on the sand, and downed a bottle of water. 'What sports do you do?' Cass asked, hugging her knees and turning around to face Saloma.

'I run and do weight training as much as I can. To be honest,' Saloma said, pushing her sunglasses onto her head, 'I haven't done anything this week and judging by the food I've been eating, I need to crank up my training once I'm back. You, on the other hand, have been consistent in your yoga and swimming.'

Cass shrugged, brushing off a sand fly from her arm. 'I grew up doing sports at school, and my mother insisted that I should take up martial arts, as she believed that girls should know how to defend themselves. Physically, that is,' Cass said, with a slight downturn of her mouth.

'So, what martial arts did you do?' Saloma asked, intrigued.

'Taekwondo and later on I took on *Muay Thai*. I also tried archery and shooting. Recently, I tried aerial and water sports. By the way, I signed up for heli-surfing tomorrow. Care to join me?' Cass asked, stretching out her legs on the sand and looking at Saloma with interest.

'Absolutely! At the starting point!' Saloma said with a laugh. 'I'll cheer you on and wait for you at the end point. I can't surf to save my life, let alone with a helicopter!' Saloma exclaimed.

Cass burst out laughing. 'Okay, fair enough. I used to have a friend who would do all sorts of sports with me. She was the only one who was game enough.'

Saloma sat up. 'Back in school?'

'Uh-huh. Seemed like a million years ago. She had great athletic abilities, and if she was in the West, she would have easily been offered scholarships.' Cass said, leaning back on her arms.

'So, what happened?'

'Her parents didn't think her sports abilities would bring her much, so she focused on her studies instead.'

'You've lost touch with her?' Saloma asked, aware that it was the first time Cass had shared a story from her life.

'Well, yes, and no. Yes, cos we did part ways at one point and no, cos I managed to find her, and we sort of reconnected.'

'Oh,' Saloma replied, unsure whether she could ask further.

'She didn't bother about getting tanned though,' Cass said suddenly.

'What do you mean?'

'Just that. She embraced the sun, the colour of her skin, her background, her culture, life in general I suppose. She was one of the few people I knew who had an independent mind, a surety, and a composure, way beyond her age,' Cass said, looking past Saloma.

'When did you meet her?' Saloma asked, curious.

Cass looked at Saloma briefly and brushed off the sand from her palms. 'Wait a second, I see a vacant lounge chair, let me drag it next to you.' Without waiting for Saloma to reply, she stood up and pulled it closer. 'I got it.' Brushing the sand off her body, she stretched out her legs with a sigh. 'Much better.'

'I should have helped you,' Saloma said belatedly.

Cass waved her hand and turned on her side, so that she was facing Saloma.

'I grew up with Ros. We were friends for the longest time. She was everything I wanted to be. Smart, sporty, funny, and strong. She was a rock and a star all rolled into one,' Cass said with a laugh. 'We spent so much time, trying one sport after the other that my mother was worried that I was getting to be a tomboy, whatever that meant,' Cass said, rolling her eyes.

'Go on,' Saloma said.

'But just like any other parent, my mother didn't bother me as long as I got straight As. Ros stayed a number of times at my place, especially during the exam period, and my mother would drive us to school the next day. People in school, started to call us Ebony and Ivory. I didn't understand at first but Ros said that life would be so boring if all of us were similar, like cookie cutters. Anyway, we continued as before and I spent a lot of time with her family too. They lived in a one room rental flat, I didn't know it back then, it being a rental and all. I only realized it later in life, not that it mattered,' Cass said with a slight lift of her shoulders. 'Her family was so rich in love that money became inconsequential, unimportant. After all, they had food, shelter, and clothes on their back.' Cass paused. 'Her mother was good with her hands and made the flat look so cosy. I spent a good part of my childhood sleeping on a mattress in the living room and reading using a torch light. In the morning, her parents would take such care not to wake up us as they had to leave at a crack of dawn to their stall at the market.'

'Stall?' Saloma asked.

'Yes, they had a stall at the market, they sold noodles and Malay kueh.'

'She was the only child?'

'Oh, she has a sister. Just as smart but more of a nerd. She preferred to read than hang out with us. Also, she was a good five years older than us,' Cass laughed.

'She's now a professor at one of the local universities.'

'So, what happened then, between you and Ros?' Saloma asked.

Cass turned on her back and studied the sky above her. 'Do you want a bite to eat? I haven't had lunch and it's nearly three,' Cass asked

'It's that late? Kind of hard to tell in this stunning scene,' Saloma said. 'Sure, I'll just have whatever you're having.'

Cass placed an order with a hovering waiter, and in between bites of fries and a burger, Cass shared that it was her father who drew a wedge between them.

'Your father?' Saloma asked, dipping her fry into the tartare sauce.

Cass nodded, wiping her fingers with a napkin.

For a good ten minutes, they ate in companionable silence.

'That was a good burger! I'm quite content now,' Cass said, hiding a small burp with the back of her hand.

'Yes, my father,' Cass repeated. 'The people in his circle told him that they had seen me too often with Ros and felt that I should widen my circle,' Cass said with derision. 'I didn't quite understand at first; I mean, what the hell does widening your circle mean to a teenager?' Cass said, throwing Saloma an exasperated look. 'Well, anyway, one day, he came home, sat me down and told me that as his daughter, I should behave in a certain way. I still didn't get it until he plainly told me that I shouldn't be seen with Ros any more cos even though she's smart and sporty, she came from a different social class. I was still confused and tried to walk away from the discussion. He called my mother but she didn't say a word, she just stood there, quiet. I only knew later as an adult, that she only did that as a form of rebellion.'

'Oh gosh. Sounds like one of those local dramas.'

Cass burst out laughing and threw a pillow at Saloma.

'You're right, it was. But it wasn't so funny when Ros avoided me at school the following days. I thought she was just preoccupied with our finals, but she was different. Distant and cool. After the exams, she took a part-time job and I didn't get to see her. I got a place in London and I heard that she received a scholarship to study at one of our local universities. It was only when I was in the third year at uni that my mother told me the truth.'

Saloma sat cross-legged and faced Cass. 'I'm listening.'

Cass hugged her knees. 'It's funny how conversations get side tracked. We're talking about food in London, and I mentioned that I missed some dishes back home. My mother then started talking about this new Malaysian café in London and how authentic the food was, but it was still not as good as Ros's mum's cooking. I was startled to hear her name; it had been a while. Anyway, she saw how upset I was and I guess she wanted to assure me that it wasn't my fault that Ros and I weren't friends any more. So, she told me the truth.' Cass paused and Saloma willed herself to wait. 'It seemed my father spoke to Ros even *before* he had that talk with me.'

'What? How?' Saloma asked.

Cass bit her lip. 'It was the day, when I told Ros to meet me at my house. I was held up in school and told her to wait for me there as it was more comfortable. Moreover, Ros knew my mum and they got along well. What I didn't know was that my father was home as well. I think he'd planned it all along. Anyway, that was the day my father told her that it was best we stop being friends. Something about how we come from different worlds. What was worse was that he offered her money. Of course, he said it was a gift, told her to buy something nice for herself or her family.'

Saloma covered her mouth.

Cass glanced at Saloma and nodded her head. 'Terrible right? I know. I was so mad that . . . '

'That you left university halfway,' Saloma finished her sentence.

'Yes. I was devastated. I took some time off and did some serious thinking.'

'That's why you took your mother's maiden name?' Saloma asked.

'It was that plus some other reason,' Cass said, a little guarded.

'So, did she take it? Your father's money?' Saloma asked.

Cass looked at Saloma in surprise. 'Of course not.'

'Oh,' Saloma said, the wheels in her head turning. 'And you said that you reconnected with her?'

'Not at that time. No. I wasn't ready. I didn't know even know what to say to her if I met her other than, I'm sorry. And then life took over and I was, well, busy and distracted. It was much later, about several years I think, that I seriously thought of connecting with her. I didn't keep in touch with any of my classmates so I couldn't ask them about her. So, I did the next best thing: I searched for her parents and went to their stall in the market, but the whole market was gone! A huge supermarket took its place. Same thing with their flat. A whole new block of flats now stood where their flat was.'

'How about her sister?' Saloma asked.

'I was coming to that. I found out where her sister worked and left messages, but she didn't call me back. Once, I even waited outside her place of work, at the university, but I lost my nerve when I saw her. The next day, I went back again, and this time, I spoke to her, but she didn't want to have anything to do with me. I even thought of hiring a private investigator.'

'You did?' Saloma said, her eyes widened in surprise.

'Yup. Don't look so surprised. It's perfectly normal to hire one. Also, I have a friend, Mavis, who is an accomplished PI, so that makes it easier.' Cass said with a chuckle.

'You do?'

'Yes. You'll be bound to meet her one of these days.'

'And so you hired her?'

'Well, no. It was all so accidental. I went to an event, about a year ago and I met an interesting woman who worked with the United Nations Refugee Agency. She was assigned to one of their field locations and was telling me about her experience and somehow Ros's name came up. Anyway, I learned that Ros was one of their best field officers, and I asked for her email and that was it.'

'And she replied?' Saloma asked.

'Not immediately. I understood. I'm not exactly a priority and with her intense job and all, well, I can't make demands,' Cass said with a wry smile.

'So what did she say?'

'Hmm . . . nothing much. Just a two-liner that she was surprised to hear from me, and she hoped I was doing okay.'

'Were you disappointed?'

'Well, a little. But she sent me another email to say that it would be good to meet up when she's back. I think it would be easier to talk in person.'

'That's hopeful,' Saloma said.

'I'm not too sure when that can happen. She's at a war-torn country at the moment. I'm just glad that I know the truth and reconnected with her.'

'She sounds like an incredible person,' Saloma whispered.

'Yes. Hey, it's getting late, we should head back to the villa. I don't know about you, but I'm so sticky.'

'Of course,' Saloma said, as she scrambled to get up. 'Cass?'

'Yup,' Cass replied, looking at Saloma with interest.

'Why did you share that story with me?' Saloma asked slowly.
'Why?' Cass frowned.

'Was it because Ros and I are both Malay?' Saloma countered.

'What are you talking about?' Cass said, raising her eyebrows.
'We talked about sports and she came to my mind. I've never
been bothered about race, never did. But I can't speak about
my community though.' Cass said, as she looked at Saloma with
an apologetic smile. 'Many of them are still hung up on racial
stereotypes and prejudices. Just look at my own father! I'm afraid
you had a taste of that during the fashion show. I'm sorry.'

Saloma bit her lip and nodded her head.

'And I know I could trust you cos you're a private person too.
And I admire your creativity, your endurance, and determination,'
Cass continued.

'You don't think I'm well . . . too driven?'

'For success? Hell, people have no right to begrudge you.
People love money. Some worship money. In fact, there is even
a God of Money. Imagine that! And take a look at the Chinese
New Year celebrations. They don't wish each other "Happy New
Year", instead it's "Hope you get rich" in Cantonese. So, you don't
have to worry about that.'

Saloma burst out laughing. 'I didn't look at it that way.'

'Anyway, you're doing what you love. How many people get
to do that? C'mon.'

Chapter 13

The ten days passed swiftly, and on the last night, Cass suggested a night in town with a few of her friends. Saloma was more than happy to dress up, put on a pair of stilettoes, and to be driven around in a luxury car. Travelling around Bali at the back of the moped had been fun, but she was tired of wearing jeans and sneakers. She was surprised and a little guilty that she didn't miss Noah as much as she thought she would. They talked every night and at times, she found him a little vague and preoccupied. When she brought it up, he brushed it off and said that he had over extended himself at the centres and was tired. Saloma had offered to cut short her trip but he was adamant that she stayed the whole duration.

Slipping into a floor-length, black, silk evening dress with a cowl neck, Saloma stood before the mirror and was glad she bought it. It was designed by a top Indonesian designer and though it was expensive, it hit her in all the right places.

She released her straight hair and let it hang below her shoulders, glad that her fringe of bangs had grown longer, giving her a sexier appeal. She wished Noah was there to accompany her, but then, he wasn't one for parties or a fancy night out. It had been a long time since they went out for dinner. She should plan one when she got home—before things got busy with Cass. It was going better than she had expected. Cass had been happy with her ideas and was more than willing to work out a business plan. Picking up her clutch purse, Saloma made way to the lobby, all too aware of the admiring glances she got from the hotel guests. One of them assumed she was from Central America, and Saloma smiled to herself.

The lobby was packed with guests, making their way to their dinner venues and the concierge was crowded with some guests annoyed that their hotel transport was late. Saloma looked around for Cass but couldn't see her. She spied a vacant chair and made her way, only too happy to let people watch. However, after forty-five minutes, she stood up and went to the front desk, wondering whether Cass had left her a message. When there was none, Saloma called her mobile phone but it went directly to voice mail. Unsure, Saloma walked around the lobby and came across the hotel bar. It was still early and was empty except for a woman who was seated at the far end of the bar counter. Saloma walked in and increased her pace when she recognized Cass. The row of earrings on her lobe glinted in the artificial light, and her strapless black jumpsuit showed off her long neck and strong shoulders.

'Cass? I've been waiting for you at the lobby. What are you doing here?'

Cass looked up and Saloma drew back in alarm. Her face was tear stained and her eye makeup was smeared at the edges.

Saloma grabbed a bar stool and pulled it closer. 'Tell me, what's wrong?'

Cass downed her drink and motioned to the bartender for another one.

'Wrong? What could possibly go wrong?'

Saloma studied Cass's profile and tried to stem her worry.

'Why don't you go without me? I've made reservations at the Rock Bar, Ayana Resort. My friends are already there including my Communications Director, Khadijah. Just ask for her,' Cass said, thanking the bartender as he appeared with her drink.

'Nah, not my scene. Let the young people enjoy themselves. I'm more than happy to sit here,' Saloma said as she lifted her glass to Cass.

'In that?' Cass said, eyeing Saloma's outfit.

'Why not. I don't think anybody cares,' Saloma said, tossing her hair.

'I think those men at that table do. Don't turn around,' Cass said as she emptied her glass. 'Would you like to continue this at the villa? I can order room service and get out of this black number,' Cass asked, signing the bill.

'You look amazing in that outfit. Edgy and badass at the same time,' Saloma said with a laugh.

'Well, apparently I'm not as badass as I thought,' Cass said, slipping off the bar stool. 'Let's go,' she said, striding ahead with Saloma close behind her.

They took a buggy back to the villa and Cass was quiet throughout the journey, staring into the darkness. Saloma felt the rush of cool air against her skin as the driver rounded the narrow tight bends without slowing down.

'He drove quite fast don't you think?' Saloma asked as they entered the villa.

'What? Was he? I didn't realize. I'll order something simple and get into my pyjamas,' Cass said as she walked to her room, tossing her handbag onto the sofa.

Saloma stared at her retreating back, feeling a knot in her stomach. Taking a few deep breaths, she quickly changed into her oversized t-shirt, scrubbed her face clean, and hung the dress in the wardrobe, caressing the soft material. Closing the door with a firm click, she tied up her hair and headed to the living room.

Cass was seated cross-legged on a padded ottoman, staring into space.

'You weren't kidding about the pyjamas,' Saloma said, eyeing the cotton blue-and-white-striped pyjamas that made Cass looked like an adolescent.

'Oh. I always have it with me,' Cass replied, fingering the sleeves. 'Ah, that's the doorbell. Our dinner is here. I'll get it.'

Saloma watched as Cass bounded to the door, relieved that she had a little of her energy back.

'Okay, thanks, just give me the tray. I'll bring it in,' she heard Cass saying to the waiter before the front door closed with a soft thud.

'Sal, I'll put the tray on the dining table, I didn't want the waiter to come in and see the mess in the living room,' Cass hollered.

Saloma looked around the room and smiled at the piles of clothing on two wicker chairs and the opened suitcases on the floor. 'Yes, that was smart,' she shouted back.

Cass returned to the living room, and sat cross-legged on the couch. 'There's salad and a soup. Is that okay?' Cass asked.

'Perfect.'

'Help yourself.'

'You're not having any?' Saloma asked with a frown.

Cass lifted her shoulder. 'I'm not hungry at the moment. I need to clear my head from all that alcohol. Water is all I need. I shouldn't have drunk on an empty stomach.'

'So, why did you?' Saloma asked, joining her on the couch, and watching her empty a bottle of mineral water.

'That's good. I was so thirsty,' Cass said as she tossed it into a bin. 'Were you close to your dad?'

'Me?' Saloma asked, startled by the question.

'Yes, were you?' Cass asked.

'Well, I guess so,' Saloma replied, trying to find the right words. 'He was instrumental in my education, taught me the importance of learning, acquiring knowledge.' Saloma paused. 'He loved movies, music and I knew he loved me. He made that pretty obvious.' Saloma shrugged. 'But I didn't share with him my deepest, darkest secret as they say,' Saloma said with a laugh. 'He wasn't home much, I always wondered about that but my mother didn't seem to mind. He has since passed away.'

'Ah, the part-time father and the full-time mother,' Cass said with a smile.

Saloma laughed. 'Yes, you could say that.'

'And your mother didn't remarry?'

'My mother? Heavens no! She's so loyal and faithful to him. Till this day, she has their wedding picture on the wall and hardly any photos of the three us or of me,' Saloma said.

'Does that bother you?' Cass asked.

'Um,' Saloma thought for a moment. 'Yes, sometimes. She makes my father more than what he was. I'm not sure whether it's for my sake or for hers.' Saloma shrugged. 'She doesn't share with me about her marriage, though I feel there was more to it than meets the eye. Anyway, he was generous with me. Bought me books. All English. Fiction and non-fiction. Lots of them.'

Cass opened another bottle of water. 'My father was overly generous. I had all the toys I wanted but he was hardly home. Poor little rich girl, huh?' Cass said, looking at Saloma with a mock sad face. 'And when he came back, I had more toys, bigger presents.'

'So was he generous with your brothers too?'

'Brothers?'

'Yes, your two brothers. The press called them the spitting image of your father. You've forgotten them?' Saloma asked with a grin.

Cass paused for the longest time. For a moment, Saloma thought she didn't hear her.

'They're my half-brothers, I'm an only child,' she finally replied.

'What?' Saloma whispered.

'Yes. The secret is out,' Cass said with a bitter laugh. 'And, they're also half-brothers.'

'You're saying that . . . '

'Yes, my father had them from two different women.'

Saloma sat in stunned silence.

'They look so alike, don't they? They don't even have a single iota of their mothers' features. It seemed like he gave birth to them all on his own,' Cass said with a hollow laugh.

Saloma gave her a quick look. 'And nobody knew?'

'Well, they do,' Cass said with a laugh. 'Their mothers do. His friends do. Maybe the press knew but didn't feel the need to publish it,' Cass said, sobering. 'Apparently, he didn't make it public out of respect for my mother. Isn't that a warped and crazy interpretation of respect.'

'Yes . . . it was. And . . . and . . . it's okay with them? Their mothers?' Saloma asked with hesitation.

'I guess so. He paid them well, I'm sure. As for the three of us, the boys and me, we grew up together, like a normal family of five,' Cass said.

'Oh. So, he got two sons from two different women, brought them home, to *your mother's* home and your mother agreed?' Saloma asked, trying to piece the information together.

'As I said, it's crazy.'

'When did you realize?'

'I sort of guessed, cos my mother hired nannies for them, but she took care of me. And every so often, their mothers would come around but my mother would always make herself scarce. And sometimes, my father wasn't around either.'

'What do you mean?'

'My father is easily distracted when it comes to women. He has the attention span of an ant. Sometimes, he used me as an excuse and brought me along with him. That way, my mother wouldn't have a clue.'

'What?' Saloma asked with disbelief.

'Yeah, that's my dad for you. He brought me along to see his other mistresses. My mother, as I said, didn't suspect a thing cos

I was with him. He bought me more toys, games, introduced me to his latest fling, forced me to call them Aunty, and made me sit in the living room while they disappeared. I lost count of the number of Aunties I've met.'

Saloma covered her mouth. 'And . . . and you didn't tell your mother?'

'At the time, I didn't know better, so I didn't say anything. And he always ended the day with a meal at my favourite restaurant, so the toys and the meal captured my attention. Poor little me, easily bought,' Cass said with a twist of her mouth.

'How old were you?' Saloma asked, horrified.

'About six years old but when I reached eight, he stopped.'

'I'm sorry, Cass,' Saloma said, reaching for her hand.

Cass took her hand away with a small smile.

'Don't be. My mother had it worse. She should have left him years ago but she stuck it through. She stood by her man just like the Tammy Wynette song. After all "he's just a man" right.'

Saloma wrestled to come up with something to say but chose to remain silent.

'Your brothers, I mean, your half-brothers, are they close to him, your father?' Saloma asked after a while.

'Huh, what? My brothers? Oh yes. They worshipped him, they still do. He spent more time with them when they grew older, when they became teenagers. Brought them for holidays and all. I was with my mother most of the time.' Cass sat up and stretched her back. 'I'm glad I didn't go out tonight. I would have fallen asleep halfway through and you would have to carry me home.'

'Rubbish, that would never happen. You would have just left early,' Saloma replied with a wave of her hand.

'Thanks.'

'What for?'

'For keeping me company. And for doing it with such sincerity,' Cass said, brushing her hand against Saloma's.

'Of course, any time.'

'Shall we eat? The food is definitely cold now,' Cass said.

'I'm really not hungry. Why don't you have your salad?' Saloma asked but Cass was no longer listening. She was deep in thought, her head downcast, picking at a loose thread on the cushion.

'He called me this evening when I was at the business centre, my father I mean,' Cass whispered.

'Oh, he did?' Saloma asked, surprised.

'He called to tell me that I have a baby sister,' Cass said with a sob.

'What? Wait, hang on, what?' Saloma asked, astounded.

'You heard me. He has a daughter from his latest girlfriend. He's so proud of his virility, a man whose one foot is in the grave, thought it was best to share it with me. His daughter. How insane is that?' Cass said, wiping the tears from her face with the back of her hand. 'I mean, what father would do that?'

'Oh my! I'm so sorry Cass!'

'Don't be! I wouldn't have bothered if he kept it to himself. I would get to know about it eventually. But for him to actually call me and tell me the news. How sick is that?'

Saloma sat unmoving.

Cass reached for a tissue and blew her nose loudly.

'My mother would have known about it and like a good parent, spared me the news but not him. *No*, he has to brag and show to the world how bloody masculine he is.'

Cass paused. 'But he has always admired my mother. She was better than him in business, she had honed her business instincts and knew which project to take. From the moment she knew his wayward ways, she started her own business ventures under her own name, albeit it with the help of her parents. So the jewellery line, your centres, and several properties belong to her and I guess, eventually to me. But my father's vast network will basically go to my half-brothers, their mothers, and who knows, who else he had fathered or slept with. I always felt that my mother was way smarter than him. I mean, even my brothers' mothers look up to her. Her relationship with them became better when they started to ask advice from her. Crazy right? Once, when I was ten, I heard them asking my mother about planning a birthday party for my father. They wanted to do it at a fancy Italian restaurant but my mother just told them, very casually in fact, that he would prefer a traditional Teochew restaurant, with all the trimmings. They agreed, and she booked the restaurant, making sure that all his favourites were available. And it was like that all the time. The power she wielded. If only she acted more on it.'

'Oh.' Saloma replied, completely speechless.

'Now, she has to live with his children, his women, and his wealth divided. She has absolutely no control over him. He has all the cards. The only saving grace is her own wealth.'

'And she never wanted to leave him?' Saloma asked, knowing the answer.

'Never! And in his way, he loves her too. At least, I know he respects her, business sense at least and often asks her for advice.'

'That's why you changed your name,' Saloma said with realization.

'Yes, I didn't want to have anything to do with him back then and still now. But I can't help his blood coursing through my veins. I'm still a part of him. It's one of the reasons why . . . I don't want to have children. His genes will stop, at least with me.'

'And um . . . marriage?' Saloma asked.

'Marriage?' Cass laughed. 'Not for me. Society has been feeding us about the wonders of marriage, parenthood, the joys of having children for decades. Yet, we see so many divorces, poor parenting, and broken children out there. Nobody talks about having a good relationship with yourself first. It's always been somebody else completing you, making you whole. That's the biggest lie. Anyway,' Cass said, reaching for another bottle of water, 'I haven't met anyone whom I care deeply about. And if I did, I don't think I need a piece of paper to prove that.'

'Oh,' Saloma said, unsure. 'And it would be okay with your mum? If you . . . you didn't marry that is?'

'I don't think she has the right to lecture me. Her success rate is zero.' Cass burst out laughing, loud empty laughter that filled the room.

Saloma rubbed the goosebumps on her arms. 'It's late, shall we get to bed?'

'What time is it?' Cass asked, looking around for the clock.

'It's about one in the morning. Our flight is at noon tomorrow.'

'We still have plenty of time. I'm not sleepy. Why don't you go ahead?'

'Are you sure? I can stay here with you?' Saloma asked, feeling a little guilty.

'You've done more than enough. I'll be okay. Positive,' Cass said at Saloma's look of worry.

'I'll see you tomorrow morning then,' Saloma said, suddenly uncertain.

'Yeah, tomorrow,' Cass said, reaching for the TV remote.

Chapter 14

'Noah! I'm home,' Saloma exclaimed, rolling her suitcase into the living room. 'Noah?' she called out, shrugging out of her jacket and walking barefooted into the bedroom. It was empty. Puzzled, she checked her handphone but there was no new message from him. On impulse, she called his number and heard a phone ringing in the kitchen. With her heart thudding in her chest, she ran to the kitchen and saw his mobile phone on the kitchen counter. There was a note underneath it. 'Gone for a quick run, will be back soon.' Saloma read the note again and turned it over, but that was all it said. She looked around the kitchen. It was clean and tidy. The kitchen sink was bone-dry and the hob looked unused.

Lugging her suitcase into the bedroom, she unpacked and placed the two shirts she purchased for him on the bed. She hit the shower and changed into one of his t-shirts, putting it to her nose, inhaling deeply before she put it over her head. Humming under her breath, she walked to the living room, only to realize that his phone was ringing. Curious, she picked it up. All it said on the screen was 'Sam'.

'Hello, this is Noah's phone.'

'Oh, um, I'm sorry, may I speak to Noah please,' a woman's voice spoke up.

'He's out for a run. May I help you?' Saloma asked, not recognizing the voice.

'It's okay, I'll call back later,' the woman hedged.

'This is his wife, are you sure I can't help you? Are you one of the parents?'

'It's fine. Thanks.'

Saloma stared at the phone. It must be one of the parents who was uncomfortable to talk to her, she thought.

The front door opened and Noah walked in, his face red and his breathing ragged.

'Noah!' Saloma exclaimed, throwing her arms around him. 'It's good to be home.'

He released her all too quickly and unlocked her arms from around his nape.

'I'm all sweaty,' he said. 'Is that my t-shirt?'

Saloma looked down at herself and nodded her head. 'I've missed you.'

He sat down on the sofa and removed his trainers, placing them on the shoe cabinet.

'You look well,' Saloma said, her eyes taking in his lithe body in running gear. 'You're looking a little tanned. Been running in the heat?'

'Uh-huh. I'm taking a quick shower,' he said, taking off his t-shirt and walking to the bathroom.

Saloma stared at his strong back and felt her stomach tighten. 'Shall we eat out? Or we can order some takeaway?' Saloma said, standing outside the bathroom door.

'I'm easy. You decide.'

'I'll just order something simple as I've gone overboard in Bali, have eaten way too much.' Saloma waited for a reply but all she heard was the shower running.

Biting her lip, she walked back to the living room and made a call to an Indian restaurant for takeaway. It would take forty-five minutes, she was told. She hoped Noah wasn't hungry. She sat down and waited for him. He came out soon enough, his hair damp and his eyes less exhausted. He ran his fingers over his jaw and Saloma could see the beginnings of the dark evening stubble.

'Feel better?' she asked.

He nodded his head and sat opposite her, on the three-seater sofa, stretching out his legs and resting his feet on the coffee table.

'We need to get a new sofa, Noah. This rattan set has seen better days.'

Noah slid lower. 'Yes, but it's comfortable. You just need to know the exact point to lean back. Like just here,' he said, leaning his head against the back of the sofa.

'You'll come home one day and will see a brand-new set,' Saloma said with a laugh.

'Well, I wouldn't put it past you,' Noah said, rolling his eyes.

'Noah! I was just joking! I wouldn't do that. I know they belonged to your parents. I would definitely discuss it with you.'

'So how was Cass? What's the latest development on your jewellery line?' Noah asked, looking at her through half closed lids.

'Cass is great! We get along so well. Honestly. I told you on the phone that we worked almost every day. I have learned so much.'

'And so . . . she will invest in you?'

'Yes! I mean, I haven't signed anything as yet but she told me personally that she's happy with my ideas and would like to start something small with me. She's working out the details and I'll have the contract by next week. If it works out, she will invest in a boutique, or atelier, or even both. We'll see. I have so many ideas, Noah! You should have seen my sketch book, I've been drawing for the entire time I was in Bali.'

Noah lifted his legs from the table and sat up straight. 'I'm glad that worked out. In fact, why don't you focus on this and leave the tuition centres to me.'

Saloma blinked. 'What do you mean? I can happily multitask. You know that!'

'I've been doing some thinking and I think it's best if I take over the centres. You need time and energy to pursue *your* dream,' Noah said.

'Noah, I don't understand. Is there a problem? Should I call Madam Khoo or the team under Chris?'

Noah paused and Saloma waited, digging her nails into her palms.

'I don't think they have a problem but I do,' Noah said, picking his words.

'So tell me!'

Noah linked his hands and studied his fingers in silence. 'I want the special programme or as Chris named it "The Genius Programme,"' Noah said with a grimace, 'to be removed. I never endorsed it in the first place. I only agreed to it when you assured me that it would be a small group of students, a niche group, but it has gotten out of hand. I have mothers calling me every day to enrol their kids in this programme. It's ridiculous! And it's not even part of my curriculum. I left teaching because of this, and you of all people knew this,' Noah said, the muscle in his jaw clenching.

Saloma stared at him and tried to quell the panic rising in her. 'Noah, Chris just gave me an update. There're only about forty students in this programme. Our teachers have been very selective and prudent. They made sure that only the ones who have the interest, the potential, *and* the aptitude to excel in Maths will be chosen. Let me speak to Chris. We can stop accepting more students, and perhaps, in the future, we could even set a number that is agreeable to you.'

'But therein lies the problem. The moment you set a target, the more determined the parents are to enrol their kids in this programme. Every parent thinks their child is a genius and with this bloody name, it's hard to explain to them the rationale behind it. Now, there is talk of favouritism, corruption, and even racism. It's getting out of hand, Sal.'

Saloma covered her mouth. 'This is the first time I'm hearing this!' she stammered. 'Are you sure this isn't just gossip, started by an unhappy mother? I'm going to call Chris now,' Saloma said, reaching for her phone.

'It's late, Sal. Nothing can be done this evening. I just feel it's not reaping any benefits.' He raised his hand. 'Okay, I know and understand that the intention behind it was good but this . . . this is what happens when you start . . . well, when you start to make class distinctions.'

Saloma stood up and sat next to him on the sofa, reaching for his hand. 'Noah, let me talk to Chris tomorrow. I'll make the changes. Why don't we stick to this present number of students and stop accepting for the next semester? We can tell the parents that we're reviewing the programme.'

Noah took his hand away and leaned forward, his elbows on his knees. 'Okay. And I want to be part of the review team. It's my school, Sal.'

'Absolutely! That will not be an issue. And I can take over all the calls that you've been having. I can speak to the parents.'

'I don't think they want to talk with you Sal. I'm the one who sets the curriculum, so they would want to talk to me.'

'Yes, I understand that Noah, but just like any other business, you cannot speak directly to all your clients when we have already put in place a proper system where staff will handle all enquiries. Parents can also liaise with the branch managers of the centres,' Saloma said with a frown. 'I don't understand. Unless . . . you . . . gave your number to a parent and she gave it to the others?' Saloma said, slowly.

'Sal, you seem to have all the answers. You're saying it's all my fault?' Noah asked, standing up.

'I'm not Noah! I'm just trying to figure it out cos it has been agreed by the team that I'll handle calls when the staff are unable to answer, and that is on a case-to-case basis.' Saloma took a deep breath and steadied her voice. 'You love to teach, Noah. So, I want to spare you the paperwork, the enquiries, or anything that disrupts your teaching. I honestly didn't mean anything by it,' Saloma explained.

Noah stood still and stared at the wall. 'Let me handle the centres. You do your jewellery line.'

Saloma grabbed his hand. 'Noah, please . . . please let me handle the running of the centres. I promise to consult you when it comes to the curriculum. I can multitask. You did say that I've a good head for business and finances,' Saloma whispered, letting go of his hand.

Noah, rubbed his jaw. 'Yes, I did say that. But it's taking so much of your time. We hardly have time together. I'm all for you wanting to be a modern wife with a career but this is too much. You're hardly home when I'm back. You've stopped cooking and we hardly have time to entertain. We've agreed not to have children and to focus on *us* but we're not even doing that.'

'But we've just started. We've just expanded the centres island-wide and we're bound to have teething problems. It just takes time. We're young and energetic. If things go well, we can retire early and explore the world,' Saloma said, her face earnest.

Noah took a seat, and Saloma watched impatiently as he made his fingers into a steeple and studied them.

'Why don't we have a nice dinner tomorrow night. It's a Saturday, and we can go somewhere fancy and on Monday, I'll discuss with Chris about the programme. I forgot to tell you that I bought you two shirts from Bali. Why don't you indulge me and wear one of them? You look so good in blue and white, I got both. Let me get them,' Saloma said, standing up.

'It seems that's all I do,' Noah said.

'What? What do mean?' Saloma asked, stopping in her tracks, but Noah was no longer listening to her, he was deep in thought. Saloma bit her lip and went to the bedroom.

Chapter 15

Noah was in better spirits when they arrived at the Italian restaurant the following evening. She was right, the modern slim-fit batik shirt showed off his wide chest and the faint gold threads in the silk shirt accentuated the brownness of his eyes. She smiled and looked around her discreetly. She noticed several women rested their eyes far too long on Noah but he seemed impervious to the looks, pulling out the chair for her. But then, he had never been vain or shown elation when he received compliments.

'You're causing quite a stir?' she teased him as he settled in his chair and reached for the leather-bound menu.

'What do you mean?' he asked, looking at Saloma over the top of his menu.

'Oh, nothing,' Saloma said, reaching for her menu.

'So, what are you having? Have you decided?' he asked, tapping the menu against the white linen tablecloth.

'I'll just have a salad and the baked fish.'

'That's all? No pasta?'

'I'm trying to cut back. I've put on a couple of pounds after Bali.'

'Really, I didn't notice,' he said, flicking out the starched napkin and laying it on his lap. A waiter came forward to their table at Noah's signal and took their order. When he left, Noah leaned forward and said with excitement, 'I've been meaning to tell you about the new batch of teachers we've just hired.'

'Oh,' Saloma said. 'About five, right?'

'Yes, five. I must say that the HR has done a good job in this regard. They're vibrant, intelligent, and have a way with kids. They just attended my training and I'm really impressed by them.'

'They've started their training? Just five? I thought we've agreed to train when we have a maximum of twenty and a minimum of ten,' Saloma said with a frown. The same waiter came over to top up their water and she was glad for the short interruption, going through the rules of the centres in her mind.

'I'm fully aware of that Sal,' Noah replied when they were alone again. 'But I'm trying out a new training method, I feel a smaller group would be more effective. I can reach out to each participant and answer all their queries sufficiently.'

'But Noah, we have procedures in place. Did you check with Chris on this?' Saloma paused as the waiter placed their starters on the table with a flourish.

'Yes, I did and like you, she was reluctant but I made her see my way,' Noah said, thanking the waiter before he left.

Saloma held her tongue and watched as Noah took a bite of his lightly seared prawns with cannellini bean mousse.

'This is heavenly! Would you like to try one,' he asked, forking a small piece for Saloma.

'No thanks. I'm quite content with my rocket salad.'

'You don't know what you're missing,' he said, wiping his mouth.

For a few minutes, they ate and drank in companiable silence.

'So, tell me about these five candidates. They're on probation, right?' Saloma asked, taking a sip of her water.

'Yes, a three-month probation, Sal. I know about that,' he said with a laugh. 'You're testing me.'

Saloma laughed. 'Well, I don't know, you've been bending the rules since I was away.'

'Hey, I wouldn't call it bending. Just a little tweaking. Anyway, these five were all former teachers with the Ministry and were burnt out just like me. They have great ideas.'

'Three men and two women, if my memory serves me right?'

'That's correct.' Noah looked up and started to tick off their names on his fingers. 'There's Nick, James, Lionel, Sam and Lay Cheng.'

Saloma's fork suspended in mid-air. 'That's four men and one woman.'

'Oh, sorry. It's Samantha. She just likes to be called Sam,' Noah said as he paused to reach for the last prawn on his plate and devoured it in two bites.

'Ah. I see,' Saloma said slowly. 'And you'll continue to train them on Monday?'

'Uh-huh. Bright and early at nine in the morning. I really enjoy this particular group. We've been meeting up even after class.'

'You mean you join them for lunches?'

'Yeah, and dinners too. Nothing fancy like this,' Noah said. 'Just at the food court or cafés.'

'With all five of them?'

Sometimes, but at times just a couple of them. Or whoever is free,' he said, signalling for the waiter. 'I need a drink. Do you want one?'

'I'm good. By the way, I don't remember you being so friendly with the trainee teachers before,' Saloma asked, raising an eyebrow.

'Like I said, they are really a fun bunch to talk to,' Noah said.

'And you've been eating out with them *every day*?'

Noah gave her a quick look. 'What's so surprising about that?'

'Well, for one, we're their bosses,' Saloma said with mock laughter.

'I don't care about labels,' Noah said with a shrug.

Saloma tightened her lips and chose her words carefully. 'It has nothing to do with labels, it's just more professional to keep a distance from the staff. We're running a business, after all.'

'Well, I don't see it that way. Anyway, I'm so used to eating out that it's nice to have some company. After all, I can't remember the last time we had a meal at home.'

'Well, I do make breakfast, albeit simple, and sometimes packed lunches,' Saloma said, a little defensively.

'I notice but they're nothing like what you used to make,' Noah said, smiling as the waiter placed his drink on the table.

'I'm working full time, Noah,' Saloma said, putting down her cutlery. 'You of all people could see that. I have to put in the hours cos it's our business. We're accountable, no one else.'

'I'm fully aware of that, Sal. But I also know that it takes time to make a business successful. We're on the right track, making enough, in fact, more than enough, what's wrong in taking some time off to enjoy our success or,' Noah paused and looked past Saloma. 'Or work maybe just three times a week?'

Saloma fixed her eyes on Noah, her body still.

'Excuse me, madam, sir, may I remove your plates?'

Saloma turned around and faced the waiter, her face red. 'I'm not done. Can't you see that?'

'But of course, madam, my apologies,' he said, and slinked away.

Saloma took a deep breath.

'Was that really necessary?' Noah said, wiping his mouth.

Saloma blinked several times and cleared her throat. 'It's impossible for me to work three times a week, Noah. I haven't even begun to start on my jewellery line and I'm all for making the centres, *our* centres a success. Yes, we've made considerable developments but we're still relatively young.' She clenched her fists in her lap. 'We've pumped a lot of capital in the business, as you know, and it will take some time before we see any profits.'

Saloma took a deep breath and tried to slow down her racing heart. Why couldn't he understand, she fumed.

'You're playing with your food,' he said, instead.

'Oh,' Saloma said, putting down her fork with a clatter.

'Let's get the mains, shall we, I can see the waiter watching us in the background.'

'Okay,' Saloma said, absently.

Noah motioned to the waiter, and within seconds he removed their plates and replaced them with their main courses.

For a moment, they stared down at the piping hot food in front of them, neither speaking.

It was Noah who broke the silence. 'I've never been that keen on the expansion but I gave the go ahead because I see your point of view,' he said, leaning back in his chair, his gaze clear and direct. 'I know it takes time but judging by the way it's going, we can make up the investment in due time. You don't need to go to the office every day. We have Chris who runs the day-to-day business. Just leave it to her and her team. All I'm asking is for you to cut back a little, to enjoy whatever success we have. Is that too much to ask?'

Saloma felt a knot in her stomach and forced herself to speak slowly. 'The staff work better when they know I'm hovering and in their faces,' Saloma said, lifting her chin. She lowered her voice. 'Noah, you can't expect me to be at home all the time. I'm not a stay-at-home wife. You know that I don't fit the traditional mould,' she pleaded.

Noah looked down on his plate of pasta and began to eat, wiping the corners of his mouth with his napkin. Saloma followed suit and took bite of her fish and though it was delicious, she couldn't handle another mouthful.

'There's absolutely nothing wrong in being a stay-at-home wife and I'm not even asking that,' Noah finally said.

'But?' Saloma asked.

Noah looked up, surprised.

'I can hear the *but* in your voice,' Saloma said, taking a sip of her cold water.

'We don't have children, yes, as we have agreed,' Noah said, holding up his hand, before Saloma could interrupt him. 'So, we *can* have the luxury to go for a holiday, to unwind and to come back refreshed and inspired. Hell, even couples with kids do that,' he said with an ironic laugh.

Saloma paused, biting her lip, and spoke with care: 'But Noah, don't you see, because we don't have kids, we can focus on our work to our hearts content. How many couples can do that? I see so many working mothers, at the gym and at the centres, permanently on their phones, juggling work, home, and kids. Half the time they're not present or focused, they're always thinking of what they should do next. Their lives revolve around a bloody checklist!' Saloma said in a rush. 'And many of them, have the temerity to tell me to my face, how good they are at multitasking! They have no idea how inefficient and ineffective they are! Sure, they get the job done but where's the attention to detail, the precision, and thoroughness,' Saloma declared. 'Look, just the other day, at the centre, I met one of the mothers. On the surface, she's a superwoman: she's a lawyer, a mother of three, and lives with her elderly parents. All good. But she's often harried, she comes in with her maid and two of her oldest children. The kids are unruly, rude and entitled. They get away with almost everything, cos the maid has no authority to stop them and the mother is permanently distracted,' Saloma said with a derisive laugh. 'It's absolutely pointless. We on the other hand, have no distractions, don't you see,' Saloma said, reaching across the table for his hand.

Noah looked down and studied their intertwined hands. 'So, what are you saying?' he said, lifting his eyes to meet hers.

'I'm saying that we should focus on our business until we reach our target.'

'And what *is* our target?' Noah asked, extricating his hand from hers.

Saloma laughed, her face alight with excitement. 'Why to make it a roaring success, of course! To prove to all those out there that we have what it takes to make this into a phenomenal success.'

'All those out there?' Noah asked, knitting his brow.

'Unlike you Noah, I still have a lot to prove, to them and to myself,' Saloma said.

'Surely by now, it doesn't matter,' Noah said with disbelieving laugh. 'And who cares what *they* think.'

'It's easy for you to say. I have to earn my place every day, every time,' Saloma said with a toss of her head.

'That's because you make it so. You overthink things.'

'That's not fair, Noah,' Saloma said, her eyes flashing. 'You know how hard it's been for me! I've told you often enough.'

'Yes, when you were younger and less accomplished and by this, I mean, according to society's ridiculous standards, but now, you're successful. There's no need for this obsessive need to prove them wrong,' he said, his voice calm and matter of fact.

'You have to be in my shoes to know how it feels, Noah. I have endured years of unfairness and prejudices. Sometimes, it's upfront and sometimes,' Saloma said with a crack in her voice, 'it's a jibe, an innuendo, or even as a joke. So, the need to succeed is stronger in me.'

'Can you understand that?' Saloma asked, brushing her eyes.

Noah pursed his lips and nodded his head.

'Look, Sal, I think both of us have lost our appetite. I'm calling the waiter to clear our plates. Is that all right?' Noah asked.

Saloma nodded and watched as the waiter dutifully came to take away their barely touched food.

'Is there something wrong with the food, sir, madam,' he asked in a horrified whisper.

'Not at all. The food is impeccable. Please thank the chef. We're just not hungry,' Noah said with an apologetic smile.

'How about something sweet? A dessert?'

'We're good, could we have the bill please?' Noah said.

'Let's go to the training centre together on Monday,' Saloma said with a sudden grin after the waiter left. 'I'm meeting Chris at ten. I can go to the office first, get an update with the Finance section, before I meet her. And by the way, Cass just told me this morning that the contract is ready, so I'll meet her for lunch.'

Noah nodded his head. He'll get over it, she thought, he always does.

Chapter 16

'Good morning, Winnie,' Saloma said as she walked through the door.

'Good morning, Mrs Salem and oh, Mr Salem as well,' the receptionist replied, startled to see both of them together.

'I'm off to the training room,' Noah said to Saloma, walking away with a wave.

'May I see the teaching schedule for this month, Winnie,' Saloma asked, leaning over the counter.

'Oh, by the way, here are copies of their resumes. From Miss Christine,' Winnie elaborated at Saloma's puzzled look. 'She said you requested for them?' Winnie said, handing Saloma a brown envelope.

'Oh yes, thanks,' Saloma said, stuffing it into her bag. 'Before I forget, I've got a little something for you, from Bali,' Saloma added, passing her a rectangular box.

'Why, thank you. May I open it?'

'Absolutely,' Saloma said as she watched Winnie slowly untie the ribbon and open the box.

'Oh Mrs Salem, this is beautiful! I've always wanted a shawl,' Winnie said, draping it around her shoulders. 'The colours are so pretty.'

'It looks good on you,' Saloma replied with a warm smile.

The main door opened, and Saloma turned her head to see a group of people walking in, dressed casually in jeans and t-shirts. They were laughing and it was obvious that they got along well.

'Those are the new trainee teachers,' Winnie said.

'Oh, are they,' Saloma replied.

'Do you want me to introduce them to you? I think you haven't met them. They came in when you're away,' Winnie said, standing up.

Saloma touched her arm lightly. 'No, some other time, Winnie, thanks. I think they're about to start their lecture.'

'Ooh, before they go in, let me tell you who's who,' Winnie said, looking up. 'The guy in the blue shirt is Mr Nick Tan, the man with the thick-frame, black glasses is Mr James Liew, the short-haired lady next to the water cooler is Miss Chang Lay Cheng, I think, and the tall lady with the curly long hair, carrying two cups of coffee is Miss Sam Tan,' Winnie whispered. 'I can't seem to find Mr Lionel Wee. I think he went to the washroom,' she said, craning her neck.

'Thanks Winnie. Miss Tan sure likes her coffee, she has two,' Saloma observed.

'Oh, one is for Mr Salem. The five of them usually have breakfast at one of the cafés, and she always gets a cup for him.'

'That's thoughtful of her,' Saloma said.

'And she's likes running too, I heard that she was an athlete in school and even joined national competitions. Sometimes, they run in the evenings,' Winnie said, going through a pile of papers.

'Oh, all five of them?'

Winnie looked up in surprise. 'No, just Mr Salem and her.'

'Oh yes, of course,' Saloma said. 'My husband did mention it. So, I'll be in the office, followed by a meeting with Miss Christine, and then I'm off to my lunch appointment.'

'Sure, Mrs Salem, and thanks again for the gift.'

Saloma made her way to the office and greeted everybody, exchanging news with those she was familiar with and showing an interest in their work, giving each of them a souvenir from Bali. She was casual yet firm and knew that the staff found her intimidating. She chatted with the finance director and was happy with the progress of the centres and invited him for lunch the following week.

'Saloma is that you? I thought our meeting is at ten?'

Saloma spun around, nearly knocking into Chris. She burst out laughing and steadied the ample woman in front of her. 'Chris, good morning! Are you okay?'

'I'm fine, thanks. What a way to start the day. Come to my office,' she said with a chuckle.

Saloma had always liked Chris. She was sensible, intelligent, and down to earth. She ran the centres with a tight leash and yet could show kindness that many managing directors fail to express. They spent the rest of the morning discussing the 'Genius Programme' and the gossip that came with it. Chris had heard of it but to her knowledge, it was only from one disgruntled mother. She promised to investigate and agreed to discuss the programme with Noah and the rest of the teachers at a later date. Just like Saloma, she felt it was wise to stop further enrolment and to suspend publicity on the programme. The meeting was better than Saloma had envisaged, and she left the centre hurriedly for her lunch appointment with Cass.

She hated to be late and drove faster than normal, relieved to find a parking space upon arrival. She hastened her steps and spied Cass through the glass windows of the chic new establishment. She waved back and walked in, unaware of the waitress running after her.

'She's with me,' Cass said when Saloma reached her table.

'Of course, Ms Khoo, we weren't sure,' the waitress muttered.

'May I have a bottle of Perrier?' Saloma asked, just as the waitress was about to turn on her heels and leave.

'Of course, Ma'am,' she mumbled and scurried back to the kitchen.

'Did she think that I was about to attack you?' Saloma asked, puzzled.

'Don't worry about it. Come here. You look well,' Cass said, giving her a warm hug.

'And you! You're rocking your jewellery,' Saloma exclaimed, studying the row of studs on her ear lobes and a Balinese-designed chain necklace around her neck.

'You like it?' Cass said, moving her head from left to right.

'Gorge! And your hairstyle really sets it off. I don't think I've seen anyone who carries off the undercut the way you do. You have a lovely head shape, and not many people can say that!'

'Oh, you don't say,' Cass said, batting her lashes at Saloma. Saloma laughed, glad to see her in good spirits. She had been different when they left Bali, quiet and reserved.

'Enough about me. Here's the contract. Study it and let me know what you think. Basically, I would like to have you onboard as a designer. I know you need a place to work, so I've created a space for you at my current store with all the tools you need. I have, at the moment, quite a number of clients who wish to engage you. You have no idea how many women have kept their family's jewellery and loathe to sell them. With you on our team, we can do so much more. I'm so excited! Each piece you make will have a story!'

Saloma looked at Cass with shiny eyes and felt a lump in her throat. She paused when her drink arrived and took a healthy swallow of the bubbly water.

'You have no idea,' Saloma cleared her throat, 'um . . . you have no idea, how thrilled I am! This is literally a dream come true for me. I'm looking forward to meeting these women and crafting pieces that resonate with them.'

'Mind you, it won't be easy. These women are entitled and used to getting their way. So, you need to balance your creativity and discretion at the same time. But I know you can handle them,' Cass said with a wink.

Saloma pushed her hair back. 'Of course, I'll do my best,' she said, fighting back tears.

'I just said that you can handle difficult clients, and here you are, about to cry!'

Saloma giggled, wiping her eyes with the edge of her napkin. 'I'm just so happy, that's all.'

'Am I interrupting something?' a friendly voice called out.

Saloma looked up and was startled to see a woman standing next to their table. She was dressed in a floral wrap-around dress that reached below her knees and her hair was loose, in shiny waves, way past her shoulders.

Cass stood up with a shriek and clasped the woman in a tight hug. 'Mavis! I wasn't sure you could come, so this is a surprise.'

'I managed to tidy up my affairs, so here I am,' Mavis replied, taking a seat, placing her top-handle handbag on the vacant chair next to hers.

'Good grief, who speaks like that!' Cass said, shaking her head. 'Oh, I'm sorry, where are my manners! Saloma, this is my friend Mavis. Mavis, this is Saloma.'

'It's a pleasure to meet you,' Saloma stammered, throwing an unsure look at Cass.

'Yes, this is *the* Mavis, I was telling you about,' Cass said with a chuckle.

'You are?' Saloma asked, surprised that Mavis looked nothing like she had imagined. She looked so feminine, so *girly*, Saloma thought in confusion. 'I'm sorry, I didn't mean anything by it,' Saloma said, feeling awkward.

Mavis laughed, a high-pitched shrill that made her cover her mouth with the back of her hand.

Saloma sat still, blinking. Good God, Saloma thought. She even laughed like a school girl. Where was the fast-talking, greasy, jean-wearing woman she had in mind?

'Well, whatever picture you had in mind when Cass mentioned me, it was definitely not this,' she said, a delicate smile on her lips. 'A glass of sparkling water, please,' she said to the waitress.

'I couldn't tell you she was coming, cos I wasn't sure, Saloma. I just thought it would be fun to connect the two of you together,' Cass said with a grin.

'So, you're a . . . ' Saloma's voice trailed.

'I'm fully licensed PI. Have been for the past fifteen years or so,' Mavis said, taking a piece of bread and breaking it into small bites before dipping it into the olive oil and balsamic vinegar.

'Don't let her feminine appearance fool you. She has a black belt in karate and Krav Maga, she's a sharp shooter, and has a master's in criminology,' Cass said.

'Don't you love to introduce me,' Mavis said with a raised eyebrow.

Cass choked on her bread. 'Actually, yes, I do. Your face is priceless, Saloma, but I've teased you enough; though all I've said about her is true.'

'I'm . . . ' Saloma stammered. 'I'm really pleased to meet you.'

'Same here,' Mavis replied.

Saloma stared at the dimple in her right cheek and shook her head. 'I would have never guessed! So, were you in the police force before you branched out on your own?'

'Yes, that's right,' Mavis confirmed, accepting the menu from the waitress.

'But don't ask her about her role in the force. It's all cloak and dagger,' Cass interjected with a chuckle.

'Yes, I can't disclose any information. I would have to make you disappear if I did and that wouldn't be pleasant,' Mavis said in a serene voice.

Saloma choked on her drink and Cass burst out laughing.

'How long have you two been friends?' Saloma asked, clearing her voice.

'About ten years,' they both chorused, before bursting into peals of laughter.

'We met at a weaving course,' Cass said, sipping her glass of wine.

'Weaving?' Saloma repeated. 'You mean the actual act of weaving something?'

'Yes, I came across this one-day course,' Cass said. 'Ooh, that's delicious,' she continued, putting down her glass. 'Um . . . I've always wanted to learn it, I had time and just signed up for it. I didn't know anyone when I arrived. It was held at a bungalow, um . . . I think, it was the home of the instructor herself, right? A fashion designer,' Cass said, looking at Mavis for confirmation to which she nodded.

'We happened to sit beside each other and over the loom machine, we started talking,' Mavis continued.

'So, what did you make,' Saloma asked, intrigued.

'I knew that was your next question,' Cass laughed.

'Oh, was I so transparent?' Saloma asked with a slight smile.

'No, silly. Cos, only a creative person would ask that. Anyway, we made coasters, you know, the ones for drinking glasses, and the next time, yes, it was so much fun that we signed up again,' she said with an impish smile. 'We made placemats. I still have them,' Cass said, looking at Mavis.

'And before you ask, I'm not a creative person, far from it. I just wanted to do something different, learn something new,' Mavis said with a giggle. 'Cass was so inspired that she went to buy herself a loom machine! I was just happy to get the finished products,' Mavis added.

'And are you still weaving?' Saloma asked, looking at Cass with admiration.

'I still do, though I need to take more classes. I've been gifting my friends with a variety of coasters for Christmas. I need to up my game,' Cass said. 'Mavis, give Saloma your name card. You've no idea when you might need her,' Cass said, throwing Mavis a cheeky smile. 'She does excellent background checks and I know many of the wealthiest ladies in this island are her clientele.'

'I wouldn't know about that,' Mavis said, passing her card to Saloma.

'Ah, she'll never tell, but I know,' Cass said with a wink.

'Background checks?' Saloma asked, looking at the simple white business card with just Mavis's name and number.

'Well, if you're unsure about a possible partner or have some reservations in hiring a staff, despite the recommendations, I can do some discreet checks for you,' Mavis said, matter-of-factly.

'Ah . . . that's quite useful,' Saloma said, turning the card over.

'Told you that it's good to have her in your phone book,' Cass said with a grin.

Saloma thought of Mavis on the way home. She had never met anyone like her before. She hummed under her breath and slowed down when she drove past the building where one of the centres was located. She peered over the steering wheel, and a surge of pride welled up inside her when she saw its name in big bold letters. Noah and her had come a long way, she thought teary eyed.

She stepped on the accelerator but braked immediately when she saw Noah coming out of the building, dressed in his running gear. She wound down the window and was about to call out when she saw a familiar, tall girl walking beside him, her pigtail swinging behind her. Saloma watched as Noah steered her to the traffic light, his hand at the small of her back. A car behind her honked, and Saloma waved to the disgruntled driver, a plan forming in her head as she joined the evening traffic.

Chapter 17

Saloma chose a corner table at the café and tried to make herself comfortable. She knew she was early but she couldn't wait at home a minute longer. At exactly 3 p.m., Mavis walked in, her saffron-coloured dress stood out in stark contrast against the oak tables and the black, leather chairs. The staccato beat of her open-toed heels against the black-and-white tiled floor caused some diners to look up and her hair was in waves just like before, but this time, she had it in a half-up, half-down style that accentuated her high cheekbones.

'You're early,' Mavis said, smoothing her dress as she sat down. Up close, Saloma took in her understated but perfect makeup.

'I know, I managed to get off early from work today,' Saloma lied.

Mavis studied Saloma with a smile. 'That, or you couldn't wait any longer to hear the news I'm about to tell you.'

Saloma tucked her hair behind her ear, a little nervously. 'Okay, you got me. Your text message made me wonder and I had to get out. Would you like a drink? Coffee?'

'A peppermint tea would be nice, but later,' Mavis said, leaning back.

'Okay, so tell me. You said that I was right to do a background check on Sam?' She had called Mavis to do a background check on Sam almost immediately after she'd seen her with Noah but she hadn't expected Mavis to get back to her so soon or find something. Saloma sat up, her heart pounding. 'And,' Saloma whispered.

Mavis nodded. 'Yes, she's quite a dark horse. She had excellent reviews from all her employers including the Ministry of Education. However, when I dug further, there was this incident which caught my eye. She did some volunteer work a few years ago.'

'She helped a number of under-privileged children run by a non-profit organization and for a while, she was really a star. She taught them Maths, Science, and English. However, there was this incident which was not reported. Officially, that is.'

'What do you mean?'

'Well, it meant that the parents, in this case the mother, did report to the social worker but it was all verbal. She did agree to a written report at first, but in the end, she claimed that it was all a mistake.'

'What was it that Sam had supposedly done,' Saloma asked.

Mavis reached for her tote bag and took out a brown folder. 'This is my report. Have a look, and I leave it to you to decide on your next course of action.'

Saloma gripped the folder and stuffed it in her bag. 'Tell me,' she insisted.

'It seems your new recruit had hit one of the children numerous times with a ruler. She stopped when the mother discovered the bruises and complained to the welfare officer. In her defence, Sam claimed that the child was hyperactive and refused to study. Of course, that was no excuse.'

Saloma covered her mouth. 'Oh my God. That's terrible! Why wasn't she reported?'

Mavis stared at Saloma for several seconds.

'No!' Saloma exclaimed.

Mavis nodded her head. 'She paid the mother a substantial sum of money. It seemed the mother was reluctant to accept at first but relented in the end cos her husband just left her. In return, she told the social worker that she made a mistake. Sam continued to teach her son, I think she didn't want to create suspicion by quitting immediately. So she stayed for a month and then left. She went for a short holiday in Europe, did some private teaching, and then applied for the job at your Centre.'

Saloma sat in silence, trying to find the right words but couldn't.

'Tea?' Mavis asked, beckoning the waiter.

'Yes, tea would be good,' Saloma said, biting her lip. She felt Mavis gaze on her and wished she could read her mind, but Mavis's eyes were veiled, discreet.

Saloma left Mavis an hour later wondering her next course of action. Her first impulse was to confront Noah with the information, but decided against it. He would be furious if he knew she did a private check on his teachers. She bought dinner and made her way home only to get a call from him that he was having dinner with his team of new recruits. New recruits indeed, she fumed.

She placed the unopened pizza margherita on the kitchen counter and got herself a glass of water. Leaning against the counter, she spied the brown envelope that Mavis gave her, poking out of her tote bag which was on the dining table. Downing the water in one gulp, she walked to the table and pulled out the two-page report from the envelope. Saloma turned the pages over several times and realized the top sheet was not printed on a company letterhead and there was no mention of her name or Mavis anywhere in the report.

In fact, Saloma thought with sudden clarity, anyone could have written it. She walked towards their desk, rummaging through the drawers, an idea forming in her head. It has to be here, she thought, going through sheafs of paper, various stationery, old batteries until she fished out a packet of unused A4 white envelopes with triumph.

She took out a piece and sat down in front of the computer, typing out Chris's name, designation, and address. With care, she inserted the envelope in the printer and checked it twice before inserting the report in it and sealing it. She deleted the document in the computer and switched off the printer. Grabbing her bag and car keys, Saloma shut the front door behind her and ran to her car. She had to mail it immediately.

* * *

Saloma bided her time, she knew it would take some time before things went pear-shaped. Two weeks later, Chris called her to her office.

'Saloma, I've some news to tell you,' Chris started. 'It's not good, I'm afraid,' she said, her smooth brow furrowed. 'Come, let's sit on the sofa, it's more comfortable,' Chris said, ushering Saloma to the cream coloured three-seater.

'Chris, this is overly dramatic. It can't be that bad,' Saloma laughed, sitting down.

'I'm afraid it is,' she replied, her face grave.

'What is it?'

'I received an anonymous letter this morning,' Chris said, almost holding her breath.

'Breathe, Chris! You're making me worried!'

Chris inhaled and continued. 'Well, the letter was about one of our new recruits. First, I wish to say that it was impossible for us to have known about this because there was no official record of it. You do know that we are very thorough in checking the résumés of our applicants,' Chris said in earnest. 'We've caught a number of applicants with fake university degrees, but this one . . . um . . . this one shocked us.'

'I have no doubt about your efficiency and your team's meticulous work ethic, so don't worry about it,' Saloma said, reaching out to pat her lightly on her hand.

'Well, I hope you still think so after what I'm going to tell you. So,' she said with a heavy sigh, 'One of our new recruits, a Miss Samantha Tan, prior to coming here, had not only physically punished a child, but also covered the offence by paying money to the child's mother.'

'What? But, Chris, surely this is just hearsay! You can't possibly believe everything you read today! It could be from a jealous colleague or just an unhappy parent,' Saloma replied. 'It's all alleged, I'm sure.'

'That's what I thought, at first. So, I called her in and asked her point blank. Initially, she denied but when I insisted that I won't report her if she told the truth, she admitted it. She claimed that it happened several years ago; the child that was assigned to her was especially hyperactive and restless. She tried several methods to gain his attention and normally, they worked, she said. But she admitted that she wasn't in a good place as her mother was diagnosed with cancer at about the same time she taught the boy. She insisted that it was just a mere tap on the child's wrist with a plastic ruler and denied causing any bruises. However, she admitted to offering money to the mother. She said she was terrified from being barred from teaching, and acted out of impulse and fear,' Chris said, tightening her lips. 'But what she doesn't know is that she'll never get a teaching job in this country ever again! I'll make sure that every learning establishment will know of her, and in time, all parents too!'

'That's terrible!' Saloma whispered, covering her mouth.

'I'm sorry, Saloma, you've entrusted me with this job, and I'll make sure this doesn't happen again. I'll do whatever it takes to check on our teachers. They're the pillars of our industry, we can't have them be abusive!'

'I know that, Chris. And have you . . . have you told Noah?'

'Yes. I'm sorry, Saloma. I planned to tell you both at the same time, but he seemed to know about the meeting and barged in.'

'What did he say?' Saloma asked, wiping her sweaty palms on her trousers.

'He didn't say anything. I think he was in complete shock. He . . . um . . . looked at Samantha and just walked out!'

'I have to talk to him,' Saloma said, standing up. 'Don't worry, Chris, you've done all that you could, and I know that you'll put in place stringent guidelines,' Saloma said, walking to the door.

'Oh thanks, Saloma. You're so kind. Thank you for understanding and being so generous with me,' Chris said with a sniff.

Saloma nodded in acknowledgement and almost ran to the car park, calling Noah at the same time, but it went directly to voice message. Muttering a curse, she started the car and careened out of the parking lot.

Chapter 18

It was one in the morning, and Saloma was lying in her bed with both the fan and the air conditioner switched on at full blast, yet sweat trickled down her back and the backs of her thighs. She gripped her handphone tight, willing it to ring. She had called as many people as she knew, but none of them had seen Noah. The last time he was seen was at the centre, and he had left without taking his handphone or his bag. Muttering a curse under her breath, she leapt out of bed and headed to the living room, feeling the wall for the light switch. The room was exactly as how she left it two hours ago, a mess—her half eaten food was still on the coffee table, there were empty plastic bottles of water littered on the floor, sodden tissues stuffed between the cushion and arm of the sofa, and coffee mugs containing dried up coffee residue on the side tables.

Ignoring the mess, Saloma paced the floor and wondered if she should call the police, but it hadn't been twenty-four hours yet. Or Mavis. Maybe she should call Mavis, she thought, wiping her face with a towel.

She heard a sound outside the front door and watched the handle turn. Throwing her phone to the sofa, she flung open the door and wrapped her arms around Noah, sobbing into his chest.

'Where were you?' she screamed, pummelling his chest.

He grabbed her two fists in one of his and pushed her away.

'Noah? Aren't you going to say something? I've been worried sick! I even thought of calling the police,' she cried out.

Noah put up his hand and Saloma stopped talking. He placed his shoes neatly in the shoe cabinet and walked to the bedroom.

Saloma followed him and watched as he took off his wristwatch and pulled his shirt out of his trousers.

'Aren't you going to say something?' she insisted.

'I'm so tired, Sal. Can't it wait till morning?' he said, sitting at the edge of the bed. His face was drawn and there were dark shadows around his eyes.

'I want to know where you were, I was so scared, Noah,' she said, clenching and unclenching her fists.

'I was at the park, sitting on one of the benches,' Noah said, pinching his nose. 'I needed to think.'

'All because of a trainee teacher?' Saloma asked, a sneer in her voice.

Noah looked up with surprise. 'Is that what you think? That's very shallow of you, Sal.'

'Okay, maybe, but she was just one of many,' Saloma defended. 'We have other teachers. What's the problem?'

'You don't get it, do you?' Noah said with a sigh and walked to the bathroom.

Saloma sat on her dressing table stool and waited for him.

'What was it that I don't get?' she asked when he came back into the room, smelling of soap and shampoo.

Noah wiped his hair and draped the towel at the back of a chair. He ran his fingers through the damp strands and rubbed his jaw. 'I'm really exhausted, Sal. Let's discuss in the morning,' he said, lying full length on his side of the bed. 'Turn off the light, please,' he said, flinging an arm over his eyes.

'No, Noah, I need to know now. I've been waiting for you since this afternoon! I deserve to know what's going on in that head of yours!'

'I'll tell you when I'm ready, Sal,' he said, turning on his side.

Saloma fought the urge to scream and dug her nails deep into the palm of her hands. She switched off the lights and slid into bed, lying on her side. It was a matter of minutes before his breathing became deep and rhythmic, and she knew he had fallen into deep sleep. She turned and laid on her back, folding her arms on her chest. The curtains were not fully drawn and moonlight filtered through the gaps, making weird shapes on the ceiling, almost hypnotic. She stared at the shadows and wondered whether she had gone too far in highlighting Sam's case. But it will die down, surely it will, she thought. And Noah will come to his senses, he always does.

Saloma closed her eyes and slowed down her breathing, willing herself to sleep. But she woke up a few moments later with a start, her heart pounding. Between dozing, she'd wake up, her chest tight and her breathing shallow. At six in the morning, she gave up the pretence completely. Carefully lifting his arm from around her waist, she got up and made herself a cup of coffee. It was still dark when she drew the curtains in the living room. She could make out the bougainvillea bushes that Noah's mother had planted years ago. Without her tender, loving care, they looked dry and forsaken. They never had gotten around to hiring a gardener.

She wished their apartment was ready; commuting would be easier and they would finally have a home of their own. But she knew that Noah was still reluctant to move. 'I grew up in the north, and I love it here,' he used to say. She hoped a developer would make him a crazy offer for his parents' home so that they could move into their new apartment with ease. He had several offers so far but none of them had moved him. They still had half a year before their apartment was ready, and Saloma knew that Noah had no qualms to rent their new apartment if he didn't get a price that he liked for his parents' home.

Saloma took a sip of her steaming coffee. Noah had never been attracted to money. The obsession to get a ridiculous sum for his parents' home was just an excuse to stay longer. He was quite open about that. But then, he had never experienced poverty, she thought. Or lived in a small flat with friends making fun of her squatting toilet or her mother's English. Saloma sighed. Despite being a minority like her, Noah had hardly experienced the oppression inherent to being one. His white skin certainly played a part, she thought.

At nine in the morning, he joined her in the living room. There were bags under his eyes, and his jaw was darkened by a day's growth of beard, but his eyes were alert.

'Couldn't sleep?' he asked, guzzling down a bottle of water.

Saloma sat opposite him and placed her empty mug on the coffee table. 'Not really. Do you want a cup of coffee? I made a fresh pot.'

'Not right now. Maybe later. I just need water.' He emptied the bottle and walked back to the kitchen.

Saloma heard him switching on the tap and refiling the bottle. 'I bought a few bottles of still and sparkling mineral water. Would you want one?'

'Nope. Tap water is fine with me.'

Saloma sat back and studied her clasped hands.

'I'm sorry, Sal. I shouldn't have disappeared like that,' Noah said, taking a seat and looking at her across the coffee table.

'So why did you? I was scared.'

'I needed to think.'

'I know, you said that last night,' Saloma said, looking at him briefly. 'So, what was it that I didn't get?'

Noah took a deep breath and spoke with slow deliberation. 'It was way simpler when we first started. We had one centre and then, three. You handled the finances and I did all the hiring of teachers. It was a good system, and I honestly enjoyed the experience.

Now, our business is spreading like wildfire. Yes, yes, I know it's good to expand,' Noah said, as Saloma was about to interject. 'Now, I'm not too sure how to go from here. Obviously now, résumés, letters of recommendations, and personal references are no longer sufficient. We need to do background checks now? How do we do that? Hire a PI?'

Saloma looked up startled.

Noah rubbed his jaw and stared the floor. 'And how do we address anonymous feedback now?' he said, looking up at Saloma. 'Do we have to believe each and every one that we get, whether it's about our staff, or *us*? I don't know, Sal. Sam said that it happened a few years ago and that she barely touched the child. It was just a tap on the wrist she insisted, but the letter seemed to say otherwise. Who do we believe? And should we still punish her when it happened years ago? Where does this end?'

Saloma sat still, barely breathing. 'You talked to Sam? When?'

'What are you talking about?' Noah asked with a frown.

Saloma cleared her throat. 'You said it happened several years ago and that Sam said she barely touched the child. How did you know that?' Saloma rephrased.

'Oh that. Yes, she stopped me as I was about to leave the centre. She was worried about her career. Is that what you took from my entire conversation?' Noah asked, staring at Saloma.

'No, no. I just wanted to be clear,' Saloma said with haste.

'So where does this end, Sal?' Noah repeated. 'And it's not just Sam we're talking about; our entire process of hiring teachers is now being questioned.' Noah stopped to gather his thoughts and continued. 'I'm also beginning to question my own judgement. I mean . . . I like this new group of recruits, I've told you often enough. I felt and *knew* they were good teachers, *good people,* now I'm doubting my own instincts, my own gut feeling. This is no longer about teaching.'

'Noah, we needn't make any drastic changes. It's just one teacher and we can easily replace her. You can do the hiring. In fact, Human Resources can invite you to sit in in all their interviews, moving forward,' Saloma said, her face earnest.

'But that's just it. I'm now moving into recruitment rather than the actual teaching. This is not how I pictured running the centres, Sal. I have to do some thinking.'

'Why don't we go for a holiday? Let's put this all behind us and go to Rome. You've always wanted to go to Rome,' Saloma said, sitting beside Noah and clasping his hand.

Noah removed his hands and stood up. 'Sal, are you crazy? Going for a holiday at this time? You still don't get it! Am I the only one worrying about the implications? Have you no idea of the enormity of the situation? We have a business teaching children. Sal, *children*. We'll lose all credibility, *I* will lose credibility if we employ the wrong teachers. I'm worried about our integrity, our entire business's integrity if this gets out the wrong way! I know I've brought up vacations before, but . . .' Noah lowered his voice and sat down again. 'Not now, Sal. I need a few days to think about this. I may need to see some of my former colleagues at the Ministry,' Noah said, running his hand behind his nape.

'I'll drive you. We'll go together,' Saloma said.

Noah emptied his water bottle and stood up. 'No, I think it's best if I did this alone. You should focus on your jewellery line, Sal. That's your baby. This is mine.'

Saloma bit her lip and watched him leave the room.

Chapter 19

'Ah, you're here. Finally, you remember me?'

Saloma felt a pang of guilt and closed the door behind her. 'I'm sorry, Mummy, I've been so busy.'

'Humph. Always same excuse. Same reason. What's this?' her mother asked, taking a bag from Saloma.

'Oh, just something small from Bali. I told you, I went there for work,' Saloma said, sitting down and wiping her brow with a damp tissue. 'It's so hot in here. Can't you switch on the fan?' Saloma asked, looking at the ceiling fan above her.

'A lot of wind coming from windows, you just wait,' her mother replied, opening the bag and taking out the items, her glasses perched low on her nose. 'What's this?' she repeated, holding the rattan coasters in her hand.

'Oh, they're coasters. For your drinking glasses,' Saloma explained to her mother's unspoken question. 'Are you saving electricity?' Saloma demanded, flapping her shirt and reaching for the fan remote and cranking it to the maximum level. 'Ah, that's better,' she sighed, leaning against the chair.

'What you doing? That's too fast! The fan is not good!' her mother screeched, reaching for the remote and switching it off.

'What do you mean? It's not working?' Saloma said in alarm as the whirring came to an unsteady stop.

'A little. I get it fix tomorrow,' her mother hedged.

'You're living with a broken fan and you waited this long to get it fixed?'

'I like the wind. All windows are opened. No problem for me.'

'I'm getting you a new fan. Maybe two: a ceiling and a standing one. I've been asking you to get air conditioners forever,' Saloma said with annoyance.

Her mother snorted. 'What for? Only for you? And you come here . . . What sometimes once in three months. Waste money.'

Saloma stared at her mother, who was dressed in a yellow pastel cotton blouse over a batik sarong, and felt like screaming.

'You look angry. I don't think it is because of fan,' her mother said, looking at Saloma with narrowed eyes.

Saloma reached for the newspapers and fanned herself vigorously. 'I'm just hot, Mummy. It's about 40 degrees out there and the humidity is like 100 percent.'

'You live here whole life. You still don't know Singapore, eh? Everyday hot.'

Saloma fanned her face and decided not to answer her mother. 'So do you like the coasters?'

'Oh, I can get that at the market. So many I see and many types.'

Saloma stopped fanning herself. 'Those are different Mummy. These are much better. Trust me.'

'I dunno, they look the same to me. So, how's Noah?' she asked pointedly.

Saloma shrugged. 'He's okay.'

'You two fight? You look thinner and,' her mother peered into her face, 'and not sleeping.'

Saloma gave another shrug.

'Marriage not good when there is no baby.'

'Mummy, not again,' Saloma moaned.

'You people don't understand. With baby, you two have something together. Focus is on baby. Now, you focus on you, and he focus on him. See my thinking. Without baby, difficult for husband and wife to come together. Man get tired, Sal, many times I said. When you fight, they move to another one. Easy-peasy.'

Saloma made a face at the common children's phrase and spoke. 'Noah is not like that, Mummy. He's different. He could have anyone but he chose me. *Me*, Mummy. I don't deserve him. You don't understand.'

'*You* make him special,' her mother scoffed. 'He no different than other man. Now, worse. No baby. No need to come back to you. Also he not Malay.'

'Huh? What on earth do you mean?' Saloma demanded.

'I said many times right, you must marry people your race. They understand your culture. Malay men always want baby, children. All one family. You become mother, take care children, husband. All happy. And you can cook. All eat same food. And if he gets another woman, he always come back because of baby, children. But you *dowan*. Everything western. English.'

'This is rubbish, Mummy. There're many Malay couples who don't want children and if they have, many of their wives worked. This is the twenty-first century for goodness' sake!'

'You wrong. All want children. You tell me who *dowan?*' her mother insisted.

Saloma wavered. 'I'm sure there are! I don't know one couple personally but I know that if I researched, I'll find one.'

'Okay, maybe one or two but not many.'

'This conversation is getting ridiculous, Mummy.'

As she drove home in the late afternoon, Saloma tried to ignore the nagging fear that Noah might get tired of her. Her mother couldn't possibly be right. She talks like a fishwife, she thought crossly. But he hadn't spoken much since his outburst. Saloma stopped at the red light and bit her fingernail. He hadn't been to any of the centres and didn't seem interested in teaching or meeting his students. When Saloma asked, he merely said that he had some thinking to do. He had taken up running in the

early hours of the morning and took his time to come home.
She had once waited for him and made breakfast, but he'd hardly
touched his food, insisting that she should proceed without him.
Half the time, he was reluctant to tell her his whereabouts, only
giving some vague answers about meeting an old colleague or a
friend. Saloma started the car and drove past a supermarket. On
impulse, she drove in. It'd been a long time since she had cooked
his favourite meal. He would love it. She found an empty lot in
the open car park and was about to get out when she thought she
saw Adeline, one of the teachers at the centre, loading groceries
in the boot of her car. She was recruited by Noah and had been
with them since the beginning. Saloma locked her car and decided
to say hello.

'Adel, hi, how have you been?' Saloma asked.

'Sal! Good to see you!' Adeline shrieked, her tanned face
breaking into a warm smile.

'Shopping for the week?' Saloma asked, taking in the bagful
of groceries.

Adeline rolled her eyes. 'Hardly, I've three boys. These will
last for three days!'

Saloma laughed. 'I don't know how you do it, Adel,
you're a superwoman. And on top of everything else, you join
marathons and win!'

'Running is my form of escapism. Nothing honourable about
it! Speaking of which, after my last run with Noah, we talked
about engaging a consultant. What do you think?'

'Sorry, could you repeat that? A truck just thundered past.'

'Noah has been joining me for our morning runs, as you
know,' to which Saloma nodded, pinning a smile on her face, 'and
after that, we treat ourselves with breakfast. A few of the other
teachers, the ones who came at the same time as me, the pioneers
as we called ourselves, joined us,' Adeline laughed. 'We're really
bumped about Sam. I mean, she was a good teacher. Anyway, we

discussed about getting a consultant. Someone who knows about our industry. And Noah knows someone.'

'Of course, absolutely, we discussed it earlier. Noah knows a few good people in the education industry, locally and abroad,' Saloma replied, glad that the last statement, was at least true.

'So, do you know this consultant? A Cassandra Webber? She's English, but she's been living here for many years. Noah said that he knew her when he was teaching and she was at the Ministry,' Adeline said as she slammed her car boot shut.

'Um, yes, he has mentioned her before,' Saloma lied.

Adeline opened her driver's door and got into the car. 'Hey, it was great catching up, at the car park no less,' Adeline said, through the window. 'I got to run! Got to feed my kids! See you,' Adeline said, driving off, sticking her hand out of the window.

Saloma responded with a small wave, her heart in her throat.

Chapter 20

Saloma entered the concrete-block building and walked into a bright lobby. A security guard sat behind a desk and looked up when she came in. Saloma gave a barely discernible nod, glad her face was hidden behind her sunglasses. She took a glance at the business card in her hand and entered a lift. On the eighth floor, she stepped out and found herself in a corridor with a row of offices on either side of her. She took her time studying each unit before stopping in front of an opaque glass door with the name 'Mavis Lee' printed in black across the door. Wiping her sweaty palms on her trousers, Saloma turned the knob and walked in, fully expecting a receptionist seated behind a desk, but all she saw was an empty and narrow carpeted hallway, save for a side table with a vase of fresh-cut flowers. Saloma turned the corner and came to a large, well-lit room. Mavis was seated behind a desk, her head bent over a ledger. She looked up when Saloma came in and motioned for her to sit down.

'Hello, Saloma. Have a seat'

'It's okay. I've been sitting all day. This is the first time I've been to your office,' Saloma said, looking around. 'I know you have an appointment at five in the evening,' she said, directing her glance back to Mavis. 'I'll try to make this quick.'

'Don't worry about it. You're looking a little pale.' Mavis said, in her usual plain-speaking manner.

Saloma took off her sunglasses and brushed her hair back. 'Nothing a few hours of sleep couldn't cure or maybe a bottle of sleeping pills,' she laughed but sobered immediately as Mavis kept her serious look fixed on her. 'I'm just tired. I can't sleep. You have a nice set up here,' Saloma said, walking around the office, studying the white furniture and the cream-coloured carpet. Mavis's desk was a modern rectangular table without drawers. Behind her were full-length windows that let the afternoon sun stream in. 'You don't have a receptionist. That was the first thing I noticed when I walked in,' Saloma said, whirling around to face her again.

Mavis leaned back in her chair, and took her time replying, her eyes never leaving Saloma's face. 'I don't see the need. Many of my clients prefer just to see me, and with modern technology, I can handle my own appointments. But I do have freelancers working for me, as and when I need them. Take a seat.'

Saloma dropped into one of the plush chairs and crossed her legs. She folded her hands on her lap and tapped her foot.

'So, what can I do for you? You mentioned in your text that you needed my help?' Mavis asked.

Saloma choked back a wave of hysterical laughter and dug her nails deep into her palms. 'I want you to follow Noah. Or arrange someone to follow him. Find out who he's meeting,' she replied, at last.

'What happened?' Mavis asked, her voice devoid of emotion.

'After the incident with Sam, he's different. He's not talking. He's not working. He goes out in the morning and is usually home late at night. Sometimes, he calls to say he's with a friend. And now, I heard, he's got this friend, a consultant, who may be helping him in the business,' Saloma explained.

'So, what's that got to do with your marriage?' Mavis asked, leaning forward.

'I think he's distracted and confused. He's not teaching, which is very unlike him and he seemed . . . ' Saloma paused. 'He seemed to have lost focus. I don't know where he goes because sometimes, he even forgets to bring his handphone. If you can help me, I can bring him back to what he loves most, which is teaching.'

Mavis picked up a ballpoint pen and twirled it in her hand. 'And this consultant is a woman?'

'Yes, she's English. Her name is Cassandra Webber. They met when he was teaching at the Ministry.'

'Right. Leave it to me. I'll keep you posted,' Mavis said, standing up, forcing Saloma to stand up with her.

'Thanks Mavis. I have an appointment with Cass so I'll make a move,' Saloma said, turning on her heel and walking away without a backward glance at Mavis. She strode to the nearest washroom and stared at her own reflection. She did look tired and pale. Damn Mavis. She rummaged for her makeup pouch in her tote bag and with deft hands, applied some colour on her pale face, and put her gold hoops back in. Studying herself in the mirror, she frowned. She released her hair from the clasp and let it loose around her shoulders. Better but not quite, she thought. She straightened her blouse and undid the top few buttons. Everything will work out. It always does, she thought and made her way to the restaurant.

It was full when Saloma walked through the doors. Hugging her handbag close to her chest, she avoided the harried waiters and diners with way too much food on their plates. Saloma grimaced. She was never fond of buffets; the dried meats, overcooked vegetables, thick gravies, and commercial desserts made her shudder. Worse, she had to serve herself. She looked around and found Cass at the far end of the room, at a corner table. She was deep in conversation with the woman next to her. Saloma threaded her way and pulled out a chair, a smile fixed on her face.

'Sal, you're here!' Cas said, standing up and giving Saloma a warm hug. Saloma returned the embrace and took a seat next to Cass.

'Am I late?' Saloma asked, looking at Cass and the short-haired woman to her left with curiosity.

'Not at all, we're early and thank goodness for that! Just look at the crowd. The queue to the fresh seafood counter is snaking all the way back to the restrooms!'

'I noticed,' Saloma said with a grimace.

'Sal, this is Deej, our Director of Communications. Deej, this is Saloma,' Cass said with a flourish.

'I've heard so much about you,' Deej said, extending a hand to Saloma. 'And I love your jewellery pieces. Can't wait to see what more you can do,' she said.

Saloma clasped her hand and took in her big eyes, framed by thick eyebrows and a short bob hairstyle which complemented her heart-shaped face.

'I've been meaning to connect both of you but never got round to it,' Cass said with a bright smile.

'Why don't both of you catch up on business, and I'll get some food,' Deej said, standing up.

Saloma was surprised to see her in a traditional Malay attire of a loose long-sleeved blouse over a long skirt.

Cass caught her glance and beamed. 'Doesn't she look beautiful! I always love it when Deej wears the *baju kurung*. They're so elegant and comfortable.'

'Perfect for buffets,' Deej said with a wink.

'In fact, I've hardly seen you in one, Sal' Cass said, a questioning look on her face.

'I'm very much into trousers, as you can see,' Saloma said, laughing at her own awkwardness.

'Well, if I have long legs like yours, I'll wear them too,' Deej said with a laugh. 'If I need to move fast, I just switch to sneakers, looks good in this too,' Deej said cheerfully. 'Right, ladies, I'll be back.'

Saloma took a sip of her drink.

'All good?' Cass asked.

'Oh, yes, of course,' Saloma said, trying to tear her gaze away from a couple who was picking at each other's food and a woman carrying two plates of seafood to her husband.

'It's terrible, I know,' Cass said, following Saloma's gaze. 'The greed is just staggering. We wouldn't be here if it wasn't owned by a friend of mine, who has been urging me to dine here. He hired chefs from all over, and I didn't have the heart to tell him that I'm not into buffets.'

'This is a new restaurant?' Saloma asked, surprised.

'I don't think so but this buffet is new, hence the crowd. Listen, let's talk about your jewellery line. I'm really happy with the way you're handling the clients,' Cass said in earnest. 'Your patience is remarkable,' she said, patting Saloma's hand. 'I have a long waiting list at the moment and some of them are not used to waiting,' Cass said with a turn of her mouth. 'So . . . I'm giving you a bigger space and I've allocated a team of craftsmen for you. I'm thinking of opening your own atelier, like soon. What do you say?'

Saloma held her breath. 'Um . . . did I hear you correctly?'

'Yes, you did!' Cass said, holding up her glass of water. 'We can celebrate another day! Today, it's all-you-can-eat buffet!'

Saloma burst out laughing and lifted her glass.

'What did I miss?' Deej said, sliding into her chair.

'I was just telling Sal that we intend to open her own atelier soon. I'm looking at next February,' Cass replied.

'Congratulations! That's fantastic. In fact, I'd like to be a client too. I have several pieces of my grandmother's that I would like to have redone,' Deej said, peeling a prawn.

'I remember you telling me that,' Cass said. 'Which one which you like to revive?'

'Definitely the classic grape diamond pendant that was popular back in the day,' Deej said with a laugh.

'Yes, I know that one! Show it to Sal! Watch her do her magic!' Cass said, throwing Saloma a big grin.

'I don't know about the magical part, but sure, come over to the studio and let me have a look,' Saloma said, fixing a smile on her face.

'Really? Well, that would be wonderful but I insist that you treat me like any other client. I refuse to accept any special treatment,' Deej said, giving Saloma an earnest look.

'Of course, silly!' Cass interjected before Saloma could reply. 'You'll get the same treatment as any other client including the price. Be careful what you asked for,' Cass said with a laugh.

'I wouldn't want it any other way,' Deej said, jutting out her chin.

Saloma nodded her head. 'That settles it then. If you're free tomorrow, drop by at the studio and I'll see what I can do,' Saloma offered, taking a sip of her water.

'That's so kind and generous of you!' Deej exclaimed, her eyes round behind her glasses.

'Not at all. Hard to refuse when my boss is sitting right here,' Saloma said with a wry smile.

'Partner. Not boss,' Cass corrected with a frown.

'But *you're* my boss,' Deej said with a wink.

'Technically yes, but you know how I hate such labels!' Cass said with a toss of her head.

'I was just kidding,' Deej said, with a laugh.

'That does look good,' Cass said, watching Deej dipping her prawn into a spicy sauce. 'I think I'll get that.'

Deej peered at the queue. 'The line has shortened. Best to go now before the crowd start to go for refills.'

'Right!' Cass said, leaving the table promptly.

'You're not having anything?' Deej asked.

'I'm not hungry. Maybe later. So, Deej is a shortened version of your name?'

'Um, yes. My name is Khadijah. My friends came up with Deej and I guess, it stuck,' she said with a laugh. 'Sometimes, my kids get cheeky and call me that too!'

'You have children?' Saloma asked, curious.

'Yes, I have two boys. I'm the only girl in the house. Actually, I have three boys. My husband is still a kid,' she said, with a smile.

'And he's in the communications field too?' Saloma found herself asking.

'Razak? The poor man has no communication skills to save his life. He's an engineer. Here, let me show you a photo of my family,' Deej said, wiping her hands with a napkin. She took her phone and passed it to Saloma. 'Here, just swipe left. This was taken recently, during a family get-together.'

Saloma obediently studied the string of family photographs of Deej, her husband, and two boys in various activities. The boys were about ten and twelve, laughing into the camera.

'They love to swim! And now, they're learning kayaking. If I don't nag at them to use sunscreen, they'd be sunburnt every weekend and that includes my husband,' Deej said, popping a prawn in her mouth.

'Okay, I'm back,' Cass announced. 'Phew, that was some battle I had to go through. Sal, have something,' Cass said, picking up her cutlery.

'I will, I'm just not hungry,' Saloma said, watching with interest as Deej spoke to the waiter in Mandarin.

'That's amazing,' Saloma said in awe.

'Isn't she? And she can write, read, and speak just as well,' Cass said, looking at Deej with fondness.

'Sorry, what did you say?' Deej asked, turning her attention to them.

'Your Mandarin was quite flawless. I mean, I have no idea what you spoke, but it sounded perfect,' Saloma said with incredulity.

'I have to thank my grandparents actually. They insisted that we, my sisters and I learned Mandarin early in life. So, I took Malay in school and Mandarin privately,' Deej said.

'That's fantastic,' Saloma murmured.

'And she even studied in Beijing for two years. I swear, she writes better than most of the people I know,' Cass said, taking a spoonful of her pasta.

'I was brought up a little different,' Saloma said. 'It was English from the day I was born. My father insisted that I spoke and read only English. See, Cass, the strategies we need to employ to tip the balance in our favour. It's not easy being a minority, we have to work twice as hard to catch-up.'

'Is that how you see it?' Deej asked, without waiting for Cass's reply.

'Isn't it?' Saloma said with a slight frown.

'Well, my grandfather may have shared your thoughts, as Mandarin was and still is an important language in this country, and he didn't want us to be disadvantaged, but for me, it was just learning a new language. I didn't think much of it. At home, my family embraced our culture and in school, I didn't feel left out or discriminated. After graduation, I was lucky to be employed by a multinational company, and after that, Cass hired me!' Deej said, looking at Cass with a smile. 'Perhaps, if I looked for it, racism, I mean, I would see it,' Deej said with a shrug. 'I tend to be more accepting, I guess. I accept my background and to be honest, I find myself going back to my roots, to my culture, tradition, and language. Maybe it's age,' Deej said with a chuckle.

'Oh,' Saloma said under her breath, at a loss. 'That's a good skill, to be fluent in different languages,' Saloma said finally, a bright smile on her face. 'Do you know any other languages?'

Deej laughed. 'Well, I'm learning French at the moment as I've always been intrigued by it.'

'Go to Paris! You've been talking about it forever. Go, before Sal's business starts next year,' Cass said, nudging Deej.

'It would still have to be during the school holidays. By the way, Saloma, my boys are enjoying their lessons at your centre. That's a huge compliment cos most of the time, I have to nag at them to go for extra classes. But ever since I enrolled them to Skills Lab, I haven't had to face any drama, so far!'

'That's kind of you. Thanks,' Saloma replied, looking at her watch.

'Got to run?' Cass asked.

'I'm afraid so,' Saloma lied.

'Hey, it was lovely meeting you, finally. Maybe we can go for coffee one of these days,' Deej said, passing Saloma her name card.

'That would be nice,' Saloma said, holding it in her hand. 'So, I'll be seeing you at the studio around noon,' to which Deej nodded earnestly. 'And Cass,' Saloma said, turning to her, 'thanks again for . . . um . . . for everything.'

'It's all you! I'm merely a vessel for you to show the world your gifts,' Cass said.

Saloma gave her a teary smile and made her way out, crumpling Deej's name card and slipping it into the nearest bin.

Chapter 21

'So this is where you work.'

Saloma glanced up from her work bench and saw Deej walking into her studio, her black pumps with rubber soles made no sound on the tiled floor. She looked different in western clothes, Saloma thought. The black trousers and the crisp white shirt completed her professional look, but somehow, she looked like any other corporate employee, ordinary.

'Is it twelve already?' Saloma asked, surprised by the sharp tone in her voice.

'Yes!' Deej exclaimed, picking up a drawing on her workbench and studying it under the light. 'Wow. You drew this?'

'Yes,' Saloma said, taking it away from Deej and putting it in a folder.

'Come let's sit at the table over there,' Saloma said, walking towards the coffee table at the corner of the room. 'By the way, have you seen the jewellery store in the front? Or the back room where the craftsmen and women work? I can give you a tour,' Saloma asked.

'Yes and yes! Many times. I work for Cass, remember,' Deej said, glancing around her with interest. 'This used to be the VVIP room. I forgot how great the lighting is in here.'

'So, can you show me your grandmother's jewellery? A pendant right?' Saloma asked instead.

'Oh yes, of course!' Deej said, opening her tote bag and rummaging through its contents. 'I know I brought it along. Give me a moment,' Deej said as she took out the contents of her bag and piled them on the table.

Saloma picked up her handphone and scrolled through her messages. She hadn't heard from Noah since he left in the morning for his run.

'There it is!' Deej cried out, placing a small purple pouch on the table. 'It was in my makeup bag all along. I knew I kept it in a special place, but in the end, I end up forgetting that special place,' Deej said, making air quotes with her fingers.

'Let me have a look,' Saloma said as she fixed a loupe over her right eye. Holding it like a monocle, she studied the grape-shaped pendant, the diamond cluster glinting in the light. 'Hmm.'

'What do you see, Saloma?' Deej asked, leaning forward.

'Well,' Saloma said as she removed her loupe and placed the pendant on a velvet tray in front of her. 'Some of the stones can certainly be reused but not all. There is some wear and tear. That is to be expected, considering how old this is. What do you have in mind?'

'I was thinking of making a ring out of this. Something prominent on my middle finger,' Deej said, thrusting her right hand to Saloma.

'Okay,' Saloma said, an idea forming in her head. 'Do you wish to wear it as it is, or would you prefer to stack it with an existing ring?'

'I see what you mean! I've seen several of my clients wearing multiple rings on one finger. But that's not me. I just want to honour her memory by wearing something of hers but with my take on it.'

'Hmm. Tell me about your grandmother,' Saloma said, reaching for her notebook.

'What would you like to know?' Deej asked, leaning forward.

'Anything you're willing to share. Just say whatever is on your mind,' Saloma said.

'Well, she was like a second mother to me. She treated me more like a daughter than a granddaughter. She was strong, loving, and motherly,' Deej said, studying her fingers.

'Sounds like a wonderful woman,' Saloma said.

'Yes, she was,' Deej agreed, looking up.

'What was your relationship like?' Saloma asked, leaning back against her chair.

'We were very close. In fact, I am what I am today largely because of her.'

'So, what do you miss about her?'

'Her voice. She had a calming voice and the way she addressed me. I guess.'

'How so?' Saloma asked intrigued.

'She didn't call me by my name.'

Saloma widened her eyes in surprise.

'Well, she did,' Deej hastened to add, 'but most of the time she just called me *nak*. It's a shorter version of *anak* or child.'

'No need to explain. I'm fully aware of what that meant,' Saloma said with mild irritation.

'I'm sorry, of course you do! It's just that, well, you speak English all the time. I forgot that you're Malay too.'

'No worries. Right. Let me think,' Saloma said, as she tapped her pencil on her notebook.

'Let's try this,' Saloma said as she made a few bold strokes in her notebook. 'We can feature the word nak like subtle typography, and I can sprinkle the reset diamonds on the letters. We can even play with some fonts, like this or even this,' Saloma said, showing her sketches to Deej.

'That's amazing Saloma! I've never considered using a word as a design. And the letters wrap around the ring, but it's so subtle.'

'Exactly. Only you can make out the letters.'

'Gosh, Saloma,' Deej whispered. 'You're incredible, you weren't kidding when you said you could bring a vintage piece to life again.'

'Hold your horses. Let me do a rendering first.'

'A rendering?'

'It's like a drawing, with all the specifics, so that both of us will be on the same page in terms of the design. Hmm, this is in yellow gold,' Saloma said, as traced the pendant. 'Is that okay with you?'

'Yes! I think yellow gold looks better on me.'

'Right. Give me some time. I'll email the drawings to you, and once you agree, I'll send you a computer-aided design. It will show the ring in 3D so that you have an exact idea of how the ring looks like. And once that's done, I'll pass it over to one of the craftsmen, and he can do the final stage of production. Is that all right?'

'Absolutely! I'm in awe. In fact, I will give you some of my mum's vintage pieces so you can work your magic all over again!'

'Let's do it one at a time,' Saloma said, feeling the corners of her lips curling into a smile.

'How about you? Do you have some great traditional pieces of your mother's?'

'Yes, one or two.'

'She must be so proud of you!'

'You'll have to ask her,' Saloma said, walking Deej to the door. 'Thanks for coming and I'll be in touch.'

'Yes, yes, of course,' Deej said, turning around to wave, but by then, Saloma was already on her phone.

Chapter 22

Saloma stared at Mavis, forcing herself to remain still. It'd been a week since they last spoke but Mavis had called in the morning, her voice neutral when she requested a meeting. Saloma had taken her time, picking out the right outfit and paying special attention to her appearance, ensuring her makeup was flawless. Yet, as she sat in the chair waiting for Mavis to start the discussion, she felt her palms beginning to sweat and her mouth starting to get dry. She straightened her back and slowed her breathing, hoping Mavis didn't notice her tightly clasped hands in her lap.

'Thanks for making your way here, Saloma,' she began, her face devoid of expression. Her hair was tied up in a loose ponytail and her dress was another wraparound, but this time it was in forest green. A dark brown folder was in her left hand.

Saloma nodded her head, not trusting herself to speak.

'We have watched Noah this whole week, he has been busy. He leaves home at six every morning and runs the same route. Halfway, he is met by Adeline, I think you know that,' to which Saloma nodded. 'They run in tandem and at about the eight kilometre mark, they stop and walk to a nearby café. They are joined by a few other people, teachers from your centres. Their discussions seem serious, and at about ten, the group breaks up, and Noah runs back home. Your colleague, Adeline, normally gets a lift back from one of the others.'

Saloma nodded. So, he spends quite some time with them, she thought. Was it so hard to share that information with her?

'May I continue?' Mavis asked.

'Of course, please proceed,' Saloma said.

'In the afternoons and evenings, he meets different people but they're usually his former colleagues. Adeline joins him sometimes. He's often in a group of three or four. However, he meets the consultant, Cassandra Webber, on his own,' Mavis paused.

'Please go on,' Saloma said, digging her nails deeply into her palms.

Mavis placed the sheaf of papers on her desk. 'Let's sit over there,' she said, pointing to the two-seater sofa in the corner.

'I'm fine, Mavis. I'm perfectly comfortable here,' Saloma insisted, relieved to have the table between them.

'All right, as you wish. I think I'll just give you a summary, and you can take this report back with you.'

Saloma nodded, wishing Mavis would just continue.

Mavis leaned back against her chair. 'He seemed to have a chemistry with Cassandra, and they talk for a few hours at a time but always at a public place; a café, a family restaurant, and even at a public park. He looked stressed often and sometimes agitated but listens to her when she speaks.' Mavis stopped and drummed her fingers on the table. 'Saloma, I honestly think there's nothing romantic or sexual in their behaviour. Once, they did meet at a hotel, but only at the lobby. That was the day she had to fly to England. She has a new position in London. So, you don't have to worry about her,' Mavis said. 'And one more thing. He also met up with Sam.'

'Oh,' Saloma said, sitting up straighter in the chair.

'She initiated the meeting,' Mavis continued. 'Yes, I know,' Mavis said to Saloma's unspoken question. 'You think she has a romantic interest in Noah?'

Saloma nodded slowly.

'Anyway, it was at a café and it was about four in the afternoon. She was early and chose a corner of the room, away from the rest of the diners. It was hard to see as it was a dark corner, but she seemed upset and cried. Noah comforted her.'

'What did he do?' Saloma asked tightly.

'He hugged her. That's all. She cried in his arms. It seemed he felt sorry for her,' Mavis said.

'But you wouldn't know that for sure or about her intentions?' Mavis paused. 'That's right, I wouldn't know that.'

'And you wouldn't know whether Cassandra has feelings for him either?' Saloma asked.

'Correct.' Mavis said with a nod.

'Sam could be manipulating him, making herself pathetic, so from feeling sorry for her, he may fall for her. And Cassandra may contact him or have a long-distance relationship with him, and you wouldn't know that either. None of us would,' Saloma insisted, her voice rising.

'Saloma, I've been in this business for a long time and I can smell a cheat a mile away but Noah . . . Noah is nothing like the men I've seen. Have you considered that he may be genuinely worried about the company's future and only meeting these people because he feels that they could help? I believe he's seriously finding a way to run the centres based on his philosophy. This situation with Sam certainly shook him, he's distracted as you say, but he's trying to find the right course of action and that could only be achieved if he talks to the right people and that doesn't include you.'

Saloma widened her eyes. 'Why not me? I've been with him since the beginning and ran the centres singlehandedly.'

'Yes, but you handled the technical part, the hardware, he does the software,' Mavis said quietly.

'But it'll sort itself out, don't you see that? It usually does. That's part and parcel of having a business. Noah is naïve and does not understand that,' Saloma said in earnest. 'But relationships are different. It requires communication and sharing of ideas! And he's sharing a lot of his ideas with other people, *other women*. He can't help it if these women fall for him! Eventually, he will be attracted to them too. It's just a matter of time,' Saloma spoke through clenched teeth. 'Anyway, thank you, Mavis. I'll get back to you.'

Saloma strode out and headed for the lift lobby, her steps quick and urgent. She jabbed the lift button and waited, pacing the carpet. Muttering an expletive under her breath, she tore open the door that led to the stairwell and ran down the flight of stairs, grabbing the handrail whenever her feet missed a step. Her sobs echoed in the dingy stairway as she made her way to her car, relieved that the parking garage was empty. She wrenched the door open and slammed it shut. Letting out a scream, she banged her fists against the steering wheel and shook it hard until she felt a shooting pain into her shoulders. Resting her forehead on the wheel, Saloma squeezed her eyes shut and allowed the hot tears to escape her lids.

Saloma didn't know how long she stayed in the car. When she lifted her head, she found a curious woman looking at her through the window. 'Are you okay?' the lady mouthed. Nodding her head, Saloma gave a wave and was relieved when she walked away, though Saloma caught her turning around a couple of times. Peering into her mirror, Saloma cleaned up her face and reapplied her lipstick. A sense of calmness had taken hold of her, and she knew what to do.

She opened the door and took the lift back to Mavis's office. She was on the phone when Saloma walked in. Motioning with her hands, she gestured for Saloma to take a seat but Saloma declined, preferring to stand, her feet rooted on the carpeted floor. She watched as Mavis spoke quietly into the phone and then ended the call.

'I didn't expect you to get back to me so soon,' Mavis said, with a slight furrow of her brow.

'Noah is lost and I need to *steer* him home, *home to me*,' Saloma said without preamble. 'I'm the only one he needs, *he'll ever need*. These women will make him falter and waver. I can't predict their actions or be privy to their intentions. Worse, he leaves me and our wealth is shared, divided. I refuse to give my wealth to some conniving witch. I've worked way too hard to just give it away. So, I want to make a new arrangement with you. I want to hire a particular candidate, a honey trapper, I believe she's called. She'll learn everything about him, through me of course, and at a suitable time will meet him. He'll see her as the perfect woman because she knows all his wants, his needs,' Saloma said in a steady voice. 'At my instruction, she'll break up with him and he'll return to me, full of guilt, shame, and gratitude as he knew I stood by him. This, I'm sure is not new to you?' Saloma asked, her head cocked to one side.

Mavis took her time answering. 'Of course not. Though some of my clients prefer a sizeable divorce settlement instead of catching their spouse in a compromising situation with an agent they hired. But you're different, you want to save your marriage,' Mavis said with a thoughtful look.

'Noah is the one for me. Always will be. He just needs me to shepherd him back. So, will you help me?'

'You must be aware that this may take months, it'll be expensive. And the results may not necessarily be to your liking,' Mavis elaborated.

'I'll pay whatever it takes. I know you can deliver, Mavis, I've done my research too.'

'There's one other outcome that you haven't considered,' Mavis said with a pause.

'Oh,' Saloma asked.

'He may not take the bait,' Mavis said.

'Oh,' Saloma said, liking the possibility. Maybe he'll tell the agent that he's married and he loves his wife, she thought, warming to the idea.

'Saloma?'

'That would save me the trouble and money,' Saloma said slowly. 'Let me know immediately of his response.'

'All right. Give me all the necessary information. I'll make the arrangement. Do you wish to see her?'

'Certainly. I'll prepare a folder for her. I don't wish to meet her here, though. Perhaps, a café or a restaurant. You decide,' Saloma said.

'Of course. You sure you want to do this? Cos there's no turning back once this is set in motion,' Mavis asked, fixing Saloma with a level gaze.

Saloma met Mavis's stare without flinching. 'Yes, I'm sure.'

Chapter 23

Saloma studied the young woman across the table as she took a sip of her drink. Her skin was clear and smooth. A light layer of blush over the apples of her cheeks and a hint of pink lipstick on her lips were the only colours on her pale, oval face. Her long hair was tied loosely at the back of her head with a red velvet clasp. Her simple sleeveless dress accentuated her slender but tall, athletic build.

Her face reminded Saloma of a flat landscape, nothing stood out. Her eyes were flushed against her face with very little crease, her cheekbones and nasal bridge were low but somehow, they complemented each other when she broke into a smile.

Her upturned eyes lit up and her wide lips parted showing small even white teeth. Saloma watched the young server's face redden when she flashed him a friendly grin.

'I understand from Mavis that you'll provide me with the necessary information,' the girl asked, her voice light and casual.

Saloma felt a twinge of irritation at her relaxed and laid-back attitude. She must have done this a million times, Saloma thought, as she kept her face blank, hiding her contempt. 'Yes. All the details are in the envelope. Everything about him is in there as well as where and when you should meet him. Get in touch with Mavis from here on,' Saloma said, as she caught the eye of a waiter and signalled for the bill.

'That's it?' the young woman asked as she watched Saloma slide a hundred-dollar bill inside the faux leather folder.

Saloma gave her a quick glance but kept her silence.

'Wait a minute,' the young woman said, as Saloma stood up to leave.

'This man. You didn't say who he is to you?'

'Does it matter?' Saloma enquired, looking down at the girl, her three-inch heels making her taller.

'Um, well, not necessarily but . . . I think it's good for me to know. I mean it'll help,' she stammered.

Saloma felt a surge of satisfaction at her discomfort and took her time answering. 'He's my husband,' Saloma replied over her shoulder and strode to the door.

Chapter 24

Saloma lifted her coffee cup to her scarlet lips and took a tentative sip. It was still hot but didn't scald her tongue as before. She hummed under her breath and looked around her. The lunchtime crowd was slowly building up in the mall. It'd been a long while since she could sit at a small café and just people-watch. The jewellery business was picking up and Noah was back at the centres teaching. Even Chris showed surprise when he resumed his duties and seemed to have put away the whole drama about Sam. Life *is* good, she thought. He came back, didn't he?

But she had to admit she'd felt out of sorts when Noah dated the agent for two months. For a while, she couldn't bear his touch and buried herself in her work; her mother's words of one woman was never enough for a man preyed on her mind, but she knew in her heart that Noah would come around. He always did.

She was proven right. Mavis had reported that their activities were innocent; long runs and lunch at mid-range restaurants. In fact, he even rebuffed the agent's romantic gestures, and was the one who terminated the relationship. She knew he would come to his senses, but he was noticeably different, Saloma thought, searching for a word as she stared into the inky depths of her coffee. He laughed less and was more factual, more matter of fact, she finally admitted to herself. It was no wonder she was both confused and surprised when he agreed to move into their new penthouse despite his earlier misgivings.

Everything had gone back to the way it was, or had it? There were times when she wasn't so sure. She caught him a number of times, staring at her, his face inscrutable but he had apologized, claiming he was preoccupied with work. And once, she woke up to find him looking down at her, his head resting in his hand, but he had jumped out of bed, before she could say anything. He must be wrestling with feelings of guilt, she thought. What else could it be?

'Saloma, it's good to see you,' a perky voice broke her reverie.

Saloma looked up with dismay when she recognized Deej. She was dressed in a business suit, a briefcase in one hand and a Styrofoam cup of coffee in the other.

'Deej,' Saloma said, standing up to give her a side hug.

'Hang on, let me put this down,' Deej exclaimed, putting her coffee cup on Saloma's table and clasping Saloma in a warm embrace.

'May I join you? It would be nice to catch up.'

'Are you sure? I wouldn't want to keep you. You seem to be in a hurry,' Saloma replied, eyeing her takeaway cup of coffee.

'No, you're not,' Deej said, pulling out a chair and unbuttoning her jacket. 'I always order coffee to go, if I'm alone. I'm one of those who hate to be at a café or restaurant by myself,' Deej confessed with a laugh as she took a seat. 'Pardon me, but I have to take off my heels, they're killing me. I don't know how you do it,' Deej said, expelling a sigh as she wiggled her toes under the table. 'This is a relief!'

'New shoes?' Saloma queried, an eyebrow raised as she sat down again.

'That's the thing. They're not! The salesgirl told me that they will soften with constant use and I've used them constantly,' Deej said with annoyance. 'I should have known better. If they're not comfortable from the get-go, they won't be comfortable, *ever*,' Deej exclaimed, reaching down to massage her heels.

'Oh, should you do this here?' Saloma asked, wrinkling her nose.

'Saloma, I can't possibly walk to the restroom at this stage. I'm sorry, I have boys at home, I've forgotten my manners,' Deej said, taking out wet wipes from her bag and wiping her hands. 'By the way, congrats. Your jewellery line is the talk of the town. I have journalists calling me, they want to interview you,' Deej said, sipping her coffee.

'I know, um, a couple of them had contacted me personally too. But, I prefer to wait until the atelier is up and running,' Saloma replied with caution.

'Really? I feel there's no harm in talking to them and having, you know, a casual conversation. Nothing serious,' Deej said. 'Even the Chinese lifestyle magazines are interested.'

'Oh, that's a nice surprise. I'll discuss with Cass,' Saloma said.

'I already did. She would have no problems with it,' Deej said casually.

'Oh,' Saloma repeated with mild annoyance. 'I'll think about it. It must be so useful to be so fluent in Mandarin,' Saloma found herself asking. 'Your experiences must be a stark contrast from the rest of us in the Malay community.'

'What do you mean?'

'Well, unlike us, your résumé is harder for *them*,' Saloma said with air quotes, 'to ignore.'

Deej tucked her hair behind her ear and shrugged.

'To be honest, I've always lived my life as how I see it. I've always believed that I'm a captain of my life, trite as it may sound. And I guess, it helps that my family is not one to talk about race. I mean, we don't live under a rock, don't get me wrong; we're fully aware we're a minority here, but my parents have never looked at it as a stumbling block. I mean, take my husband for an example, he's got a Masters in Engineering, was top of his class all his life, but when he's out in the field, many assumed that he's a technician or a construction worker and not the chief engineer.

Why? Because of his skin. His "golden hue", as he called it,' Deej said with a giggle.

'He joked about it?' Saloma asked with incredulity.

'Well, he could rant and rave but what's the use? The best was just to laugh,' Deej said. 'The acute generalization only shows their ignorance and they often apologize in the end, not always, but sometimes they do,' Deej elaborated.

'But wasn't it your grandfather who asked you to learn Mandarin? Wasn't that one of the ways he taught you to beat the odds?' Saloma countered.

'As I said before, perhaps, but I don't think he did it out of anger, or how should I put it, as a one up, it was more to learn a new language. He learned Japanese during the Second World War. No one asked him to. So, I guess, he applied the same principle with us. Also, I'm always interested in learning a new language,' Deej said with a laugh. 'How about you? You married outside your race. So, your experiences would also be different,' Deej said, looking at Saloma curiously.

Saloma took her time to answer. 'Well, my father, as I've mentioned before, always drummed into me the importance of the English language, so I've always been aware of its significance. I guess it became natural for me to gravitate to the English-speaking crowd at an early age. On reflection, this was a blessing as I got to meet Noah. He's so unlike any other person, I've met.'

'But surely inter-racial marriages are common today. And I don't think it's because of language. I think love is the unifying factor,' Deej said with a wink.

'Well, I can only speak for myself,' Saloma said, as she lifted her chin. 'It's definitely a common language, that brought us closer. Of course, there's love, but how can you have love, if there's no understanding?' Saloma leaned back against the chair and spoke with mock humility. 'You know, I could have taken the easy route and married someone in our community but, well, I'm like a square peg in a round hole, as they say. Unlike you, I'm not accepted by our community *or* the Chinese. Either way, I'm screwed. So, I have to work harder than normal. I guess, no one can understand my struggles, the complications I have to go through. But it's paying off. I've got my business, Noah has his, and soon, we'll be moving to our first home,' Saloma said with a smile.

'You are? I was under the impression that you're already in your marital home,' Deej said, stirring her coffee.

'No, not yet. We stayed at his parents' home since we got married. They were getting frail and Noah thought it was best if we stayed with them. It's been several years now. But they have since passed. Anyway, I found this fantastic apartment in town with an incredible view! We could see Johor from our balcony. One of my clients, introduced me to her interior designer and she's helping me. I need all the help I can get,' Saloma said with a laugh.

'That's sounds fabulous,' Deej said, slipping into her shoes. 'By the way, I received the 3D computer graphics of my ring! They're gorgeous! Please proceed with the production,' Deej said with excitement.

'It turned out quite lovely, I have to admit,' Saloma said with a smile. 'I'll let you know once it's ready.'

'Please do! I can't wait to show it to my family. I think I better go before Cass sends out a search party for me,' she said, standing up and smoothing her skirt. 'I'll keep you posted about the interviews,' Deej promised as she stumbled out of the café.

Saloma gave a small wave and looked down at her mobile phone as it rang. Her lips widened into a broad smile when she saw Noah's name; all thoughts of Deej instantly disappearing from her mind.

Chapter 25

Saloma hummed under her breath as she patted the whole chicken dry with a paper towel. Throwing the kitchen towel up over her shoulder, she mixed the dry spices of coriander, cumin, fennel, chilli, black pepper, and salt with a little water into a paste. She massaged the paste over the whole chicken, making sure that every crevice was covered with the fragrant concoction. It was Noah's favourite roast chicken marinade. A vibrant departure from the usual black pepper and salt rub, he'd often told her. Saloma smiled. She couldn't wait to see his face when she served it to him, complete with a side of roasted potatoes in clarified butter; crispy on the outside and soft on the inside. Swaying to a popular tune playing on the radio, Saloma laid the chicken on a baking tray and tucked wedges of lemon and half a bulb of garlic around it. She slid the tray into the preheated oven and checked the time on the kitchen clock. She had more than enough time before dinner. It would be their last meal at the house. The renovations at their penthouse were completed, and it was even more beautiful than she had expected. Noah didn't appear as exuberant as she was when they viewed the apartment a few days ago, but he seemed content to sit by the balcony. He was never drawn to material things, Saloma thought, but she loved that he always indulged her.

The front door opened and Saloma looked up in surprise. 'Noah, is that you? You're early!'

'Yes, the meeting ended earlier than expected,' he said, dropping his crossbody bag onto the floor. 'I smell something familiar,' he said, sniffing the air.

Saloma wrapped her arms around his neck and smiled into his face. 'It's your favourite dish sayang, roast chicken with my special rub.'

'Is it tonight, the special dinner you talked about?' Noah asked, moving easily out of her embrace and walking towards their bedroom.

'Um . . . yes, you do remember right?' Saloma asked with alarm, following him closely from behind.

'Isn't it tomorrow?' Noah asked, lifting his eyebrows as he stepped into their room.

'It was initially but I had to reschedule cos I have to see my mum tomorrow. I reminded you the day before yesterday,' Saloma explained, hands on her hips, standing by the door.

'It must have slipped my mind,' Noah said over his shoulders. 'I've been bogged down with recruitment and updating the syllabus. In fact, I have to meet some of the teachers tonight to ask for their feedback,' Noah said, as unbuttoned his shirt and shrugged it off, dropping it into the laundry basket.

'Why don't you see them tomorrow, instead? It's perfect as I'll be with my mum,' Saloma said as she watched him standing in front of the open wardrobe, bare-chested.

'Hmm . . . what did you say?' Noah asked as he studied the row of shirts, whistling under his breath.

'I said, why don't you reschedule it to tomorrow?' Saloma said, trying to hide her annoyance.

'Sal, I'm sure you wouldn't want me to disrupt the schedules of *six people*. Many of them have kids,' Noah said, giving Saloma a quick glance. 'They would have made prior arrangements for a caregiver tonight. It's just dinner for the two of us, we can have it another day. What's the problem?'

Saloma balled her fists and lowered her voice. 'I've made your favourite dish, Noah. It's already in the oven. You've always said that I hardly cook, so I planned this meal for us. After all, it will be the last dinner we have in this house. We're moving in the weekend. I hope you remember that?' Saloma asked in sudden panic.

'Of course, Sal. Why wouldn't I?' Noah said, as took out a short-sleeved, white shirt.

'Well, you did say that you've been busy and all . . . ' Saloma's voice trailed. 'By the way, thanks for everything,' Saloma said with a bright smile as she approached him.

'For what?'

'For agreeing to move to the apartment, for indulging me when I wanted to upgrade to a penthouse and now, to moving in. I'm also so grateful that you gave me a free hand with the renovations and furnishings. I hope you liked the big reveal? The design and decor of the new apartment I mean,' Saloma elaborated. 'I made sure everything was perfect before you came in. You have no idea how hard I pushed the contractors and the interior designer,' Saloma said, buttoning his shirt.

'I can button my own shirt, Sal.' Noah said, removing her hands. 'As for the move, well, I guess it's about time. My parents wouldn't want me to keep this house for long anyway,' Noah said as he tucked his shirt into his trousers. 'As for the decor and furnishings, well, I can see your hand in it, your style.'

'What do you mean?'

'Just that. It's definitely your style,' Noah said.

'But do you like it?' Saloma asked, suddenly unsure.

'It's fine. Anyway, I've found a buyer. A buyer for this house.'

'You did?' Saloma asked in disbelief.

'Yes. Someone introduced me to a developer and we started talking.'

'Wait a minute, *You* met a developer?'

'You make me sound like I live under a rock, Yes, I met a developer, and he was talking about this area and was excited when I told him that I owned this property.'

Saloma tried to clear her head. 'But Noah, who introduced you to this developer? Was it Chris or Madam Khoo?'

Noah frowned as he ran a comb through his hair. 'I think it was Adeline. Anyway, he's very legit, cos I met Madam Khoo, and she had nothing but good things to say about him.'

'You discussed this with Madam Khoo and not with me?' Saloma asked, feeling hurt.

'Don't be such a baby. He met me a few weeks ago. I think, it was the time when you were busy with your clients, and I didn't want to disturb you. So, I did my own research, and I only talked to Madam Khoo just recently, when she dropped by at the centre,' Noah said, picking up his sneakers. 'I'm sharing it with you now,' Noah said, turning to Saloma.

'Of course, I just thought that you don't like to do business, and you've always said that I've a good head for it,' Saloma finished with a pout.

'You absolutely have a better head for business than me, hands down, but this property belonged to my parents and now, me. I should be the one to handle it. It's my responsibility.'

'I would have loved to help and join in the discussions,' Saloma added. 'So,' she said brightly, 'did you get a good price?'

'More than I could've possibly imagined. Hence, I agreed to the sale. He's going to build a low-rise private condominium,' Noah said, sitting on his haunches to put on his shoes.

'That's amazing! We can expand and invest more into our centres. I've always felt we need a second training centre, preferably in the northern district. I'll talk to Madam Khoo about it!' Saloma said excitedly.

Noah looked at Saloma in surprise. 'No Sal. I want this to be separate from the business. I'm sure you can understand that. I mean, it's their hard-earned money. I have to think how best I can honour them.'

'Oh, so you won't put it in our joint account?' Saloma asked, confused.

'I can't Sal, it wouldn't be right. I hope you understand,' Noah said as he looked at his watch. 'I have to go. Thanks for cooking today. I'm sure we can eat it tomorrow? Oh, we can't as you're meeting your mother,' he said, pursing his lips. 'How about sandwiches, instead. I'm sure you can pull it off.'

Saloma looked up at him, eyes wide. 'Um . . . yes, yes, of course.'

'Great! Don't wait for me,' Noah said and slipped out of the front door.

Chapter 26

Singapore 2010s

Saloma entered the photography studio quietly and shaded her eyes from the glare of artificial light coming from the three-light setup. Her sneakers made no sound as she made her way to Cass who was looking at a monitor and speaking softly with a bearded man.

'How's it going,' Saloma whispered to Cass when she was done.

Cass barely turned her head, her eyes fixed on the scene in front of her. 'So far, two of the makeup girls have left crying, several designer pieces sponsored by Dior are torn, one of the interns has up and left, and the photographer is trying his best to manipulate the lights because these women want flawless photos of themselves but yet, insisted on looking natural. Other than that, we're good,' Cass said through gritted teeth.

'Right,' Saloma said, giving Cass an astonished look. 'But they seem all right,' Saloma said, watching the two women, Mrs Ivy Lee and her grey-haired mother, gamely following the instructions of the photographer.

'Humph . . . this is their twentieth take! And don't let that sweet looking woman fool you. She was the one who made the makeup artists, in plural mind you, burst into tears!' Cass said, giving Saloma a quick look.

'You don't mean Ivy? Why she's lovely,' Saloma replied in surprise.

'Not her, her mother, the eighty old woman posing beside her.'

'Oh, you mean . . .?' Saloma's voice trailed

'Yes! Don't get me wrong, Sal. I love your idea of capturing these remodelled jewellery pieces into a brochure; it's a homage to the past and a celebration of modernity but getting these women together is a nightmare! We can make a reality TV show of these cock-ups! I have a strong urge to just feature the jewellery and ditch these women!'

'Cass, please don't! They provide the human element to the story,' Saloma whispered back. 'And their stories are so fun and exciting!'

'I'm beginning to think that they're either made up or totally exaggerated,' Cass hissed.

Saloma couldn't help smiling.

'Why don't I take over, I'll talk to them,' Saloma pleaded.

'Sal, your powers are many and mighty but they're not limitless. I have to bring out the big guns, this time.'

Sal looked at Cass in amusement. 'This is getting very dramatic. Who do you have in mind?'

'My mother! They'll only listen to her! And I also need diversity, Sal. At the moment the brochure is the who's who in Singapore. I know, I know, it was my doing,' Cass interjected as Saloma was about to interrupt. 'I felt that it was good to start with them, but I didn't think they would drag their friends along. A testimony to your creative skills, Sal!' Cass said, looking at Sal with a mixture of admiration and annoyance. 'How about you and your mother?'

'What about me and my mum?' Saloma whispered back in astonishment.

'To be featured as well. I've devoted an entire page on you as you're the designer, but it would be nice to have a little story about your mother too. After all, you did refashion some of her jewellery pieces.'

Saloma took hold of Cass's elbow and steered her out of the studio.

'Where are we going?' Cass said with a laugh.

'It's so hard to talk in here,' Saloma said, opening the door and leaning back against the wall. 'Cass, it was lovely of you to think of my mother but she hates dressing up and worse, being photographed. I have other clients that we can feature. Let me look at the list again.'

'That's good. Have a look at your list again. I know you've met a diverse group of people. I want this brochure to reflect that. We also need to feature ordinary women, those who were not born with a silver spoon in their mouths,' Cass said tightening her lips. 'Hopefully, with my mother's help, we can still launch your atelier on schedule.' Cass expelled a breath. 'I find this so exciting. Exciting for you!' Cass said, looking at Saloma with a beaming smile.

'Without you, I wouldn't even be here, Cass. So, thank you, for making this possible,' Saloma said, looking at Cass with fondness. They have grown closer over time and though Cass never did share the details of her family with Saloma again, there was an unmistakable bond between them.

'Hey, by the way, I'm sorry that we couldn't make it to your housewarming party. Mum and I had to make a trip to Bali, one of our investors called for a meeting. Anyway, I was told that your apartment is fabulous with an enviable view!'

Saloma shrugged. 'It's all right.'

'But?' Cass asked.

'There's no but,' Saloma replied with a laugh.

'There sure is,' Cass insisted, looking straight at Saloma.

'It's nothing. Nothing really,' Saloma said. 'Well,' Saloma continued with a toss of her hair, 'I wish Noah felt the same way.'

'Did he say he didn't like the apartment?'

'To be fair, he hasn't said anything negative about the apartment, or the view. It's just that he doesn't say anything.' Saloma pursed her lips. 'He seems preoccupied and sometimes, well, sometimes . . . a little tense.'

'Have you spoken to him about it?' Cass asked.

Saloma burst out laughing. 'You can't make Noah talk when he doesn't want to. Wild horses wouldn't be able to pry anything from him. It's okay. It's just all the changes we have been through, especially in the expansion of the centres. He will understand once he sees the benefits.'

'Yes, I've heard about the proposal of building a preschool under his name,' Cass said.

'Isn't that a fantastic development? I couldn't believe it when Lee mentioned it. Of course, it's all talk at the moment,' Saloma said with restraint.

'Noah is so lucky to have you,' Cass said with a grin.

'You think so?' Saloma asked.

'I know so! You're an inspiration, Sal. A trailblazer. Don't you know that? How many women have done what you've done? Not one. You remind me of my mother,' Cass said with seriousness.

'Really? You don't think that I'm too ambitious?' Saloma asked.

'Hey, this is the twenty-first century, we can do whatever that makes us happy. By the way, if you're a man, you would be seen as focused and driven. Don't let small minds bring you down. I'm serious,' Cass said looking at Saloma intently. 'Look at my mum. She fought hard to get where she is right now. You or I, have more opportunities than her. Use that. Don't let social norms define you.'

'Thanks Cass,' Saloma said, blinking.

Chapter 27

'Mummy, I'm back,' Saloma said, closing the door behind her.

'I can see that,' her mother responded, turning off the television.

Saloma raised her eyebrows. It was not like her to switch off her favourite Malay drama.

'Don't let me stop you from watching,' Saloma said in surprise.

Her mother snorted. 'Stop me? That's a recording. My second time watching it.'

'You can record local dramas now?' Saloma asked, taken aback.

'Of course. Who's living under a rock now?' her mother asked, throwing back the exact line she often used at her.

Saloma burst out laughing. 'Touché, Mummy. I deserve that!'

'You so pale. You sick? You look better with a little colour,' her mother declared, giving Saloma a run down.

'There's no pleasing you,' Saloma said, settling down on the sofa. 'If I'm too tanned, you asked me to be indoors, and when I'm too pale, you claim that I'm not well.'

'Humph. You don't look healthy to me. And you look thin, maybe even a little skinny,' her mother said, looking at her hard.

'Okay, Mummy,' Saloma replied with a sigh. 'I look terrible. I get that. I'll try to look better the next time I come.'

'You always so sensitive. Defensive.'

'How're you, Mummy?' Saloma asked instead.

'I'm okay. As if you care,' her mother sniffed. 'Last time you came, was two months ago. You think, old woman like me can't remember?'

'I was busy, Mummy, and I've never said that you're old or forgetful as you just implied.'

'Busy with business or problems with marriage,' her mother asked, narrowing her eyes.

'With work, Mummy,' Saloma said with a start.

'You always say work,' her mother said.

'Well, it is. What else can it be?' Saloma replied.

'I saw your Noah in the papers,' her mother said suddenly.

'You read the English papers?' Saloma asked in astonishment.

'You think I can't read?'

'Mummy, who's being defensive now,' Saloma asked with weariness.

'Okay, you right. Mr Lee showed me the *Straits Times*. He explained to me. He said Noah is rich. So, how much is enough for you?' her mother asked, leaning back against the armchair and using a hand-held paper fan branded with the words *Giant Supermarket* to cool herself.

'What do you mean, how much is enough?'

'Well. Money of course.'

'Huh? How do you link the article with money,' Saloma hedged.

'Always think I stupid, I don't know better.'

'Mummy, here we go again, it's been barely five minutes!'

'Mr Lee said Noah is very rich. He also know your centres. His grandchildren like to study there,' her mother replied instead.

'It's funny you listened to your friends and not me. I've been keeping you posted all these years,' Saloma replied with annoyance.

'I know. I remember. But they remind me. So, how much is enough?'

'I don't know, Mummy. I don't think there's a limit. You just work hard and see how it goes.'

'Hmmm. Money is good to have. Give security. But not happiness.'

'I think I'm pretty happy, Mummy,' Saloma said, closing her eyes and lying back against the back of the sofa.

'I made fish curry today. I still have some more. Do you want some?'

'It's okay, Mummy. I'm not hungry,' Saloma replied, not opening her eyes.

'Eat more vegetables, Sal. Fruits. Water. You eat too much cheese, milk, and bread.'

'What are you now? A nutritionist,' Saloma asked, opening one eye.

'That's what the doctors say,' her mother said. 'You must know. You cleverer than me.'

Saloma sat up and increased the speed of the ceiling fan. 'It's so hot in here. I wish you'd allow me to install an air conditioner in this flat,' Saloma said, flapping her shirt. 'Well, at least, you got the fan fixed,' she said, looking up at the whirring blades. 'The last time, it was spinning like crazy.'

Her mother shrugged. 'Yes, I repaired it. It was free too. The RC helped me.'

'RC? Oh, you mean the Residents' Committee. That's nice of them,' Saloma said, leaning back again.

'They nice only when the MP is coming,' her mother said with a sniff.

'Does he come often?' Saloma asked. 'I think I saw his photo at the lift lobby and in the lift itself.'

'Aiyah, his face is everywhere, markets, schools, shops. All over. Big banners; photos with residents, always same smile. He comes once a month, but during elections, every day,' her mother sniggered.

Saloma smiled. She could see her mother chatting with the politician, showing none of her current disdain.

'By the way, your neighbour on the third floor, the lady with the green parrot; she's back in Malaysia to see her sister, right?' Saloma asked, curious.

'Yes, why?' her mother asked, sitting up.

'I thought I heard a female voice when I walked past but it wasn't her. The woman didn't sound local. Strange. But I heard her husband's voice though, that I'm certain,' Saloma said with a frown.

'Oh,' her mother said, as she resumed to fan herself.

'What do you mean, oh,' Saloma asked.

'I think the voice was massage lady. They come to your house now. You only have to pay more. They bring massage table too.'

'He has massages at home? But isn't he retired, and about seventy plus?' Saloma asked with a raised eyebrow.

'Massage is massage, nothing to do with age,' her mother said with a thoughtful look about her.

'Oh,' Saloma said with a laugh. 'Well, I hope his wife knows. I haven't heard about this massage woman when his wife is around.'

'With man, it's like flying a kite,' her mother said.

'Huh? What are you talking about now?' Saloma said with a burst of laughter.

Her mother shrugged. 'This was what my mother told me and her mother told her.'

'Okay but what does it mean?' Saloma said, rolling her eyes.

'So simple. With man, you must be clever to know when to pull the string hard and when to release it,' her mother said, giving Saloma a pointed look. 'But if you smart, you can release and give freedom. Or, you make him think so,' her mother said, leaning back.

'Was that how you treated Pa?' Saloma asked, stunned.

'None of your business, Sal,' her mother said with a slight irritation in her voice. 'He was good man. Always come home. Even late at night. Always think of us. Gave us food, money. What more I want?'

'How about being loving and true to each other,' Saloma asked, looking at her mother straight in the eye.

Her mother returned her stare and shook her head. 'You young people make marriage so . . . complicating.'

'What do you mean?'

'You make marriage,' her mother paused, searching for a word. 'Difficult, or very stressful. Every time must prove love for each other. Must say I love you, every day,' her mother said with a loud belly laugh.

'What's wrong with that?' Saloma asked, annoyed.

'Too much. Cannot breathe,' her mother said, cupping her hands around her neck.

'You're exaggerating,' Saloma said with pursed lips.

'I speak truth. It's you who don't like it. Now women want flowers, dinners. I saw on TV, women get angry when men forget wedding date, birthdays, *aiyah*, all so silly. And now there is . . . what you call it . . . date night?' her mother asked, looking at Saloma questioningly. 'Why? You married already, have children, and then go for this . . . date night?' her mother asked with another shake of her head.

'Because couples need to get away from the kids. They also need to connect with each other,' Saloma spluttered.

'That's why it becomes too complicating. Like I said. You young people make, what is the word,' her mother said, looking past Saloma, 'you make standards so high.' Her mother brought her hand up to make a point. 'Not possible, sure fail.'

'Well, I supposed your marriage was perfect, happy?' Saloma asked, lifting her chin.

'You silly girl. Nothing is perfect. Why must marriage be perfect?' Her mother looked at her and spread her lips into a wide smile.

'What's so funny?' Saloma asked, irritated.

'You,' her mother said with a laugh. 'Always defensive.'

'That's because, you're always attacking me. Making me feel less than I am!' Saloma said, tightening her lips.

'It's you who think so,' her mother said with an air of calmness. 'I don't do nothing. You make yourself feel like that.'

'Really? So, you're always right? Never at fault.'

'I don't understand what you say,' her mother said.

'How convenient of you,' Saloma said, standing up.

Her mother shook her head and continued to fan herself. 'You like this with Noah? Always make answers in your head?'

'Well, if you're not honest with me, how can you blame me for drawing conclusions on my own,' Saloma shot back.

Her mother looked at her and then looked away.

'Answer me!' Saloma shouted.

'Why you shout? So rude.'

'I can't stand your one-liners! How did Pa ever stand you! You're judgemental, self-righteous, and supercilious!'

'Ah . . . now, you use big words. To make me feel stupid. Maybe you speak Malay? You don't even try. At least, I try to speak English.'

'Oh you understand all right! I'm sure of that,' Saloma spat out.

Her mother fanned herself. 'Your Pa came home. All the time. Stayed with me. Till the end. How about your Noah?'

'What do you mean?' Saloma screamed. 'My Noah comes home to me all the time too!'

'How long you together. What ten years. Still new. Now he comes home. *Later?* Five or ten years later? You work, he work. Both independent. Both have money. No children to share, to care. Told you to marry Malay men. They always want children. Your Pa and me together for forty years. Long, long time. We understand each other.'

'Noah loves me!' Saloma retorted, her face red with effort.

'Yes, but does he need you? Myself,' her mother said with a shrug, 'I only housewife. No money. So your Pa must care for me.

He knows he is father and husband. He knows I need him. And I take care of him. Make him happy. All the time. So, he needs me too. To be mother. To be wife. We both a team.'

'We're a team too! Noah and me. We even have a business together!' Saloma cried. 'Nothing to say to that?' Saloma said, incensed by her mother's stillness. 'C'mon. Suddenly, you have no opinions?'

'Man and wife never should work together,' her mother finally spoke. 'No freedom. No space. Again can't breathe. Big mistake, Sal. I promise you. You think you are together but actually no. So, you and Noah, not team. You don't need each other. Nothing to make him stay. What is important: to need each other.'

'What do you know about *my* marriage? You've never been interested in *my* life or what I do. And now, you're giving me advice? From your *own experience*,' Saloma sneered.

Her mother lifted her shoulders. 'I always try to make you see. But if you don't like, it's okay.'

'How kind of you,' Saloma said, curling her lip. 'And all the time, whilst I was growing up, Pa was away three quarters of the time, and it wasn't cos of work, that's for sure!'

'I told you, with men, it's like you fly a kite. You must give freedom. Make them happy. Then they come back. You make them feel special. Make them happy again. Happy to come home. Be with you. Then you hold string tight. Remind them family. Responsibilities. Like your Pa. Come home every time. Always. He even died in this house. I was by his side. How about your Noah? You sure he can do that?'

'You're hateful!' Saloma screamed, heading for the door. 'You're nothing but a horrible mother, do you know that!' Slamming the door behind her, Saloma headed for the stairs, breathing hard. Grabbing the handrail, she descended the steps, two at a time, until she forced herself to stop. Placing her hand on the wall, she steadied herself with her eyes shut tight. With a muffled sob, she sat down on the steps, oblivious to the dirt and the smell of urine. Was her mother right? Noah did have everything. And with his money and looks, he could have any woman he wants, just like Cass's father. She needed to have a greater level of control, Saloma thought. She couldn't be like Cass's mother who was at the mercy of her husband's philandering ways. Maybe the ridiculous kite analogy wasn't so stupid after all.

Taking deep breaths, she rested her hot forehead on her knees and waited for her heart to slow down.

Chapter 28

'Saloma, is that you?' Mavis asked, her voice rang loud and clear across the line.

Saloma cleared her throat, 'Yes, um . . . yes, it's me, Mavis. Is it convenient to talk?'

'Give me a moment.' Saloma heard a door shut, and a chair creak as Mavis sat down.

'What can I do for you?' Mavis asked as she came back on the line.

'I was wondering if we could meet up, perhaps somewhere other than your office, or a café?'

'Hmm, it's five in the evening at the moment, I was hoping to go for a run. Perhaps, we can meet up at the park, near my place? Do you know Bishan Park?'

'Bishan Park? Of course. Is that where you live?' Saloma asked, surprised.

'Well, close enough but I do like to run there. I know a few benches that are hidden from prying eyes near Bishan Car Park A, off Ang Mo Kio Avenue 1.'

'Sure, I can meet you in forty-five minutes thereabouts,' Saloma said, looking at her wrist watch.

'Perfect,' Mavis said.

Saloma ended the call and started her car, making her way out of the car park. It could be her last time visiting her mother, she thought, gripping the wheel tight for a second. Stepping on the accelerator, she ignored the pedestrian crossing and sped through, weaving in and out of the traffic with one hand on the steering wheel. She had always known her mother was different from other mothers. Growing up, she had found it confusing that her mother wasn't affectionate: she didn't hug, kiss, or even hold her hand. She remembered trying to clasp her mother's lax hand when she was about six years old, but it wasn't long before her mother released her grip, with curt instructions for Saloma, 'to keep up' or 'stay close'. And when she took her time, crossing a traffic light, her mother reached for her wrist or elbow but promptly let it go the moment they reached the other side. Then it was back to, 'keep up' or 'stay close, Sal'. On the rare occasions they hugged, it was never a full embrace. It was always an awkward forty-five degree angle before her mother stepped away, almost as if the act itself would set her ablaze. But neither did she hover like most of the mothers she knew. As far back as she could remember, her mother didn't make a fuss about her schoolwork, grades, or activities. In fact, while her friends had to stick to a curfew, Saloma was able to move freely as long as her mother knew where she was.

What set her apart from the other parents, Saloma thought, biting her lip, was her dogged ability to keep Saloma at arm's length; a steadfast refusal to be too involved in her life. For the most part, Saloma had accepted it. In fact, her mother's lack of curiosity didn't undermine her ambition, on the contrary, it spurred her and spared her from her mother's rituals and rules. But on this occasion, she was different, Saloma thought, tightening her lips. This time her mother was deliberately cruel, with the sole objective of hurting her. Saloma wasn't sure she could get past this, she realized with sudden clarity as she entered Bishan Park. Reversing into a lot, she switched off her engine. She was early. Winding down the window, she leaned back in her seat and closed her eyes. But as hard as it was to accept, Saloma knew that her mother had a point about Noah. He had to *need her*, to know that she was the only one, the only one he'd ever need.

'You've been waiting long?' a voice broke through her reverie.

Saloma opened her eyes and found herself face to face with Mavis, who had stuck her head into the open window. Her face was scrubbed clear of makeup and she kept her hair in a ponytail under a black cap. She looked more a like a teenager than an accomplished professional, Saloma thought in a daze.

'C'mon out,' Mavis said, moving away from the car. 'And wind up your window.'

Saloma scrambled out of the car and winced as her heel caught in between the concrete cement slabs on the car park driveway. 'Damn! Why do they insist on installing these,' Saloma muttered, bending down to dislodge her heel.

'Wait, let me do it,' Mavis said, kneeling down. 'Hang on to me,' Mavis instructed.

Saloma obeyed and balanced herself on Mavis's shoulder, surprised to see her in a muted black t-shirt and shorts.

'You're all in black. I miss those vibrant colours I often seen you in,' she found herself speaking out loud.

'Stand still, there you go, it's freed,' Mavis said, standing up, dusting her hands. 'I hope you have a pair of sneakers in your fancy car?' Mavis asked, raising an eyebrow.

'I sure do,' Saloma said, as she went to the back of her car and unlocked the boot.

'Here, hang on to my shoulder as you change shoes,' Mavis repeated, standing close to her. 'That's better,' Mavis declared with approval before she strode off.

'Hey, wait for me!' Saloma said as she slammed her boot shut and ran after Mavis.

'What's the rush?' Saloma asked, as she kept pace with Mavis's strides.

'Rush? There's no rush,' Mavis said as she kept her brisk pace and avoided with ease, the joggers, cyclists, mothers with toddlers and headed to a quieter area, away from public eye.

Saloma followed Mavis closely, keeping the low hanging branches away from her face. They came to a quiet clearing and Saloma spied a wrought iron bench in a corner.

Mavis brushed off several dried leaves from the seat and motioned for Saloma to sit down. Saloma gingerly sat down next to Mavis and only when she was comfortable did Mavis start to speak: 'Come, tell me what's the urgency.'

Looking into Mavis's questioning eyes, Saloma forced herself to speak in a slow deliberate manner: 'I want you to hire another girl; a better one. One who could ensnare Noah, captivate him, and when the time is right, break his heart. Really break his heart. This time, I want him to realize that I am the only one he needs, he *ever needs*.'

Mavis held her stare and spoke without missing a beat. 'I don't understand. Why are you doing this again? Hadn't he proven to you from the last assignment that he wasn't interested? In case you've forgotten, it was *he* who broke off with my agent and he's back with you. Isn't that what you wanted?'

'I'm well aware of that, Mavis. But I don't think she was good at her job. Hire a different one instead.'

'She was good. I can assure you. I can certainly engage another woman but explain to me why you need to do this again?'

Saloma watched a common rose butterfly flutter away from a bougainvillea bush and spoke with care. 'Yes, he's back but it's just not the same. I noticed it, especially after the housewarming party we held recently. He's quiet but tense and sometimes watchful. He doesn't share as much; not that he did a lot in the first place,' Saloma said, giving a quick glance to Mavis, 'but it's for sure, less now and well, um . . . usually when it comes to finances and business matters, he'll consult me.'

'And now he doesn't? Did something happen?' Mavis asked.

'Well, he sold his family house without even telling me. That's pretty big cos normally, I would be one doing the leg work.'

'But isn't it his property and thus, his responsibility?' Mavis countered.

'Of course. He said the same exact thing but I just sense that it's different this time.' Saloma hesitated. 'And there're also small little things that I notice.' She thought back to the nights he chose to watch the sports channel rather than come to bed with her, and slept on his side when he finally came to bed in the early hours of the morning. Or when his eyes didn't light up when she called him 'sayang', the only Malay term she gave herself permission to utter, just because it sounded unique, rather than the ubiquitous 'darling' or 'honey'.

'And you think by hiring another woman, it will change him?' Mavis asked, breaking Saloma's thoughts.

'Yes,' Saloma said matter-of-factly.

'This is a dangerous game, you're playing. You're aware of it, right?' Mavis asked to which Saloma nodded. 'It may drag on for months, with no end in sight, or it can end with him falling for her irrevocably, or third, they may fall for each other instead. In other words, I can't promise you a result you desire,' Mavis said without blinking.

'So, I repeat, get a different agent, someone who isn't quite so professional.'

'What do you mean?' Mavis asked, for once, looking surprised.

'Well, Noah is used to women falling for him, not that he cared.' Saloma fingered her wedding band. 'I guessed that's why he's so attractive to women. He's not conscious of the magnetic pull he has. But he can spot a fake a mile away. *So,*' Saloma said, her voice hardening, 'get an agent who is a little gauche, a little insecure, someone who has not done this before but needs the money desperately. And I don't care how much it costs, just get it done.' Saloma returned her stare.

'You want an amateur to do this?' Mavis asked, widening her eyes.

Saloma weighed her words. 'Well, yes and no. I just don't see him being interested in someone who is polished, out for a kill, so to speak. He has to be captivated and curious. So, when she breaks his heart, he will be devastated, hurt. Only then, he'll realize that I'm the one for him.'

Mavis studied her hands, and Saloma wished she knew what she was thinking.

'Normally, I wouldn't argue with a client but I think there are other options you should consider, Saloma,' Mavis, finally spoke. 'For example, take a break, go for a holiday, get reacquainted with each other. If that fails, go for couples' therapy, I know a few good ones.'

'You're kidding right?' Saloma asked with a twist of her mouth. She stared at Mavis's deadpan face and gave a short laugh.

'You don't know Noah, do you? He's not like any other man who could be coaxed by a fancy holiday with all the bells and whistles. And therapy? Can you see him sitting on a couch, spilling his heart to a stranger and then magically, all is well? Honestly, Mavis, I thought better of you!'

'Both have been proven to work, Saloma,' Mavis replied quietly.

'Yes, for ordinary couples, but not for Noah, and definitely not for *us*. Can you imagine Noah in therapy? Hell, I don't think I can even drag him to go, for one,' Saloma said with a snort. 'He has issues in articulating his feelings to me, what makes you think he will do so with an unknown person?'

'They are trained specialists,' Mavis countered.

'Doesn't matter. It's still a stranger!' Saloma replied.

'And how about spending some time together? It doesn't have to be a holiday at a romantic hideaway. Just take a week off and enjoy each other's company. Do those activities that create laughter and joy. I'm sure you can do that at least?' Mavis persisted.

'Now? When my atelier is about to launch and we're in talks of expanding the centres to epic proportions? It's impossible. Don't you understand, Mavis, you cannot push Noah, he has to realize on his own that I matter. *Only me.* It will take time but I'm willing to wait, to make the sacrifice,' Saloma replied with a calmness that surprised even her.

'If he's as special as you say he is, why do you need to go to all these lengths?' Mavis asked with a sudden look of curiosity in her eyes. 'Aren't you treating him like any other ordinary male who could be ensnared by a woman?'

'You don't know much about men, do you Mavis?' Saloma asked, turning around to face her directly. She paused and bit her lip. 'But thank you for asking me the hard questions; for treating me as more than just a client. However, I know what I'm doing,' Saloma said, touching Mavis's arm lightly. 'Just do as I ask. Please. You have all the information you need. I want to see this woman, as you know.'

'As you wish. I'll keep you posted,' Mavis said as she stood up. With a nod, she walked away, leaving Saloma alone with her thoughts.

Chapter 29

'Noah, I'm home! Where are you?' Saloma demanded, kicking off her heels and flinging her handbag onto the leather sofa. She heard the television and walked down the hallway to the den. The door was closed but she could hear the voice of the football commentator through the door. 'Noah,' she called out as she turned the knob. He was lying on the chaise lounge, eyes glued to the game. An ice-cold bottle of water was on the coffee table, condensation running down its side and seeping into the black lacquer finish.

'Noah!' she repeated, reaching for a coaster in one of the drawers and placing it under the bottle.

'Noah!' she called out, reaching for the remote.

'Hey,' he said, looking up at her with a frown before turning back to the screen. 'Give it back.'

'I need to talk to you. It's important,' Saloma insisted, tapping the remote against her hand.

'Can it wait until after the game?' he said, reaching for the bottle of water, his eyes never leaving the screen. 'Goal!' he yelled, standing up and punching the air with his fists. 'That's how it's done!'

'Please, I need to speak with you,' Saloma said, blocking his view with her body.

'All right, all right. Give me the remote,' he said, lying back on the lounge.

Saloma slapped the remote into his open hand. He looked up in surprise but didn't say a word.

He pressed the pause button and leaned back, his legs crossed at the ankles.

'It's a bloody recording!' Saloma bristled.

'Yes,' Noah said. 'What is it you want to talk about?'

Saloma swallowed her irritation and stood in front of him, hands on her waist. 'I just met Lee, earlier, and he told me that you spoke to him *last week* about declining his offer of opening a premium preschool? Please tell me that he's mistaken,' Saloma said, enunciating every word with precision.

'Yes, I did tell him. What about it?' Noah asked, lifting one shoulder.

'What about it?' Saloma echoed in disbelief. 'Well, for one, I felt incredibly stupid going on and on about this . . . this phenomenal opportunity he has given us, only for him to tell me that you rejected it! And you told him this one week ago. *One week*! And you didn't see the need to share this with me? Since when do we do things without consulting each other!' Saloma finished, her eyes flashing.

'Why are you acting all surprised. I told you after the housewarming party that I wasn't keen on it.'

'Yes, but you didn't reject it either!' Saloma shot back.

'I'm not comfortable entering into a project that I have no expertise or experience in,' he answered, looking at her in the eye.

'But Lee will engage someone with the proper credentials, your name will attract the best there is! That's the whole idea!' Saloma said, clenching her fists.

'But that will confuse the public wouldn't it?' Noah asked.

'No it won't. We will be transparent about it and say we are partnering with someone who has the right expertise because we feel the need to reach out to more students!' Saloma insisted.

'Do you hear yourself?' Noah asked, his voice soft.

'What on earth are you talking about?' Saloma asked, her face flushed red.

'You sound like an entrepreneur who wants to have a finger in every pie,' Noah said, linking his hands behind his head.

'That's not true! I'm thinking of our future, I always am. We have to grow and expand,' Saloma said with a huff.

'We have expanded. We have grown. But you want more. You always do.'

'What's wrong with that? If I were a man, people would say that I'm indefatigable, enterprising, but just because I'm a woman, I'm what . . . greedy, obsessive, or even . . . power hungry,' Saloma spat.

'I didn't say that. You did.'

'But why didn't you tell me?' Saloma repeated.

'I didn't have the chance. You've been busy preparing for the launch of your atelier, and I happened to meet Lee, that's it.'

'But we're a team. Couldn't you have warned me?' Saloma asked, swallowing her fury.

'It's my baby, as you often told people,' Noah said, looking at the television.

'But still!' Saloma insisted.

'I don't interfere in your jewellery line, do I?' Noah said, turning to face her.

'No you don't, but we started the centres together and *I* run the centres. You teach. That's has been our arrangement,' Saloma said, refusing to back down.

'It's no longer feasible. Your atelier is about to be launched. You don't have the time and I want to focus on running the centres, I can teach any time,' he finished smoothly.

'This is the first I'm hearing of it,' Saloma said, astonished.

'Well, I'm telling you now,' he said, uncrossing his legs.

'And you didn't just happen to meet Lee. He told me that you called him and invited him for drinks,' Saloma accused.

'If you really want to know; I signed up for a talk, and the day before the event, I discovered he was one of the speakers. I called him and invited him for a drink after the talk. He accepted, and I told him the truth. That's it,' Noah said with a shrug.

'But what a wasted opportunity,' Saloma wailed.

Noah emptied the bottle and reached for the remote. 'Not to me,' he said, with finality. 'By the way, your mother called me. Twice. Something about you ignoring her calls.'

'Oh. I've been busy,' Saloma hedged. It was true. She'd not been picking up her mother's calls. It'd been two months since she ran out of her flat, and she was in no mood to see her any time soon.

'It's best you tell her yourself,' Noah said, settling back against the cushion and playing back the recording.

Saloma stared at his carved profile and opened her mouth to speak but changed her mind. She closed the door shut and leaned against it with her eyes closed.

Chapter 30

Saloma stood before the full-length, leather-framed mirror in the hotel suite, and felt a frisson of excitement; all her hard work was finally paying off. She blotted her crimson lips with a piece of tissue and smiled at her reflection. It was happening. It was *the* day. She was officially a full-fledged jewellery designer with her very own atelier. Who would have guessed that someone like her, growing up in a small flat, could achieve all this success. She took a deep breath and closed her eyes. It took her exactly 365 days from the moment she met Cass to this historic moment, of standing in a six-star hotel suite on a Saturday morning, waiting for the launch of her atelier in barely an hour at the hotel lobby. Saloma felt a small shiver. But what if it failed? Her eyes flew open. What would happen to her relationship with Cass? She was not merely a business partner but also a friend. Saloma suddenly felt sick. She stepped away from the mirror and sat down on the soft, cube ottoman.

'Are you ready?' Cass asked, coming out of the bathroom, a playful smile on her glossy lips.

Saloma stood up on wobbly legs and adjusted her hair. 'Do I look all right?'

'You look sensational! And you know that, you don't need me to convince you. This is *your* day, the day you've been waiting for!' Cass said with a laugh.

Saloma looked at Cass's beaming face and took a deep breath. 'Thanks, Cass. You made this possible. I know, I know,' Saloma said with a grin, 'I've said this a million times and you would then say that it's all me, but honestly, as creative as I am, this launch wouldn't be possible if you didn't believe in *me*, invest in *me*,' Saloma insisted.

'Nah, with your talent, somebody else would have noticed you. It was just a matter of time,' Cass said with a shrug.

Saloma blinked several times and tried to laugh.

'Hey, don't ruin your makeup, and mine too,' Cass said, dabbing her eyes.

'You look wonderful, Cass,' Saloma said, looking at the petite figure in an off-the-shoulder, fitted, white jumpsuit. 'And your hair,' Saloma said, reaching out to touch Cass's short pixie hairstyle which showed off the new undercut hair tattoo on her nape clearly.

'I know,' Cass said, looking at her reflection with a chuckle. 'My hairdresser has surprised even herself,' Cass remarked, turning to the side to get a better look of her nape.

'I can never pull it off,' Saloma declared with reverence.

'Why should you? You're a goddess in your own right! By the way, I didn't see Noah. Is he coming later?'

'Um, yes, yes, of course!' Saloma replied with a fixed smile. 'He has a meeting he couldn't get out of. He'll be here later, when all the journos have left. He just hates to be interviewed, you know that, and he wants the press to focus solely on our opening,' Saloma said, digging her nails into her palms. It wasn't entirely untrue, Saloma defended herself. He did hate to be interviewed or worse, misquoted.

'That's a good man, for sure!' Cass declared. 'Speaking of journalists, let me check with Deej whether they're here. I better go down and have a look. Knowing Deej, she has probably wined and dined them, especially those social media influencers,'

Cass said, with a shudder. 'Anyway, that woman can work miracles! I'll be back. By the way, I saw the ring you made for Deej. It's beautiful. She's been wearing it every day since she collected it! What a clever idea! I couldn't make out the letters until she pointed it out to me,' Cass said over her shoulder as she hurried out of the room. Saloma smiled. She had to admit, the ring was one of her favourite pieces.

She looked around the spacious hotel room suite, decorated in classic Italian design, and let her fingers trail over the upholstered sofa and curved armchair. Having the atelier located at a premium hotel lobby certainly has its perks but she knew it wasn't easy to secure a unit. She recalled the frustrations Cass and her mother endured before the lease was finally signed. And the work didn't stop there, there were delays in the renovations, delivery of furniture, and eventually working on the actual launch. It was Deej who suggested a soft launch rather than a grand opening, as they could invite a select few and work towards making a bigger impact. They could control the outcome, she insisted. Saloma had left it to her and Cass, knowing that Cass had her best interests at heart, and focused primarily on the jewellery. But it was harder than she thought it would be; designing and overseeing the centres, both at the same time, became an exhausting juggle.

In fact, the last six months had been a blur, she had to admit, picking up a hairbrush that a stylist had accidentally left behind and making a mental note to inform Deej. It was Noah who told her one morning to leave the running of the centres to him and Chris. In fact, his insistence took her off guard, but she'd relented, knowing it was the right decision. But the long hours kept them apart, more than she anticipated. She knew from Chris he had taken a more dominant role in the running of the business and had stopped teaching. Curious, Saloma had asked him when they crossed paths one morning. 'Teach? When do I have time to teach, Sal? I will, once your atelier is up and running,' he had said with a frown. Yes, that was it, she thought with sudden realization. He was more decisive, assured, less of a teacher, and more of an entrepreneur. She stroked the salmon pink roses on the coffee table, and knew he wasn't lying when he said he was busy.

Mavis had given her a full report of his whereabouts and it often ended with him staying late in his office, alone. She knew he had met with the agent but Mavis had assured her that it was still in the early stages. So far, it had only been lunches and the occasional dinner at a restaurant. Saloma studied her face in the mirror and tucked her hair behind her ear, watching the diamonds studs catch the light. The agent, Saloma mused, a neutral term that Mavis often used, and one that she readily accepted, was younger than she had expected. There was an innocence about her that was quite attractive, even beguiling. Saloma bit her lip. Perhaps, she *was* playing a dangerous game. Has she gone too far? Saloma rubbed the goosebumps on her bare arms and drew in a sharp breath. What would happen if he found out? But how could he? Mavis was best of the best, she thought with a renewed sense of confidence.

'Sal!' Saloma heard the door open, and Cass came in, a huge grin on her face. 'Come,' Cass said, pulling Saloma by the hand. 'It's time for you to make your grand entrance.'

'Cass, it's not just me, it's the both of us!' Saloma demurred.

'Don't be coy! It's all you. Come.'

Saloma allowed herself to be led by Cass to the elevator. It *was* her day, Cass was right. Straightening her shoulders, she stepped off the elevator and greeted the guests, smiling into the camera as the bulbs flashed.

'Is this what you mean by a select few?' Saloma asked Cass under her breath, still smiling.

'Yup, you better get used to this. It's going to be bigger and better from now onwards,' Cass replied, as she broke away from Saloma and greeted a few of the guests.

'Sal, Sal, congratulations! We're here!' Saloma looked up and saw Su-Ann waving at her, Janice by her side, looking like two peas in a pod.

'Su-Ann, Janice, thanks for coming,' Saloma said, looking at them with a smile.

'Thanks for having us! We love everything in your atelier and this recycling ideology. In fact, we found a few pieces that we like, but the price is way, way above our budget,' Su-Ann declared, widening her eyes. 'How about giving us a discount? After all, we send our kids to your centres and most importantly, we've been friends forever,' Su-Ann smiled, rolling the 'r' for good measure.

'Why don't you show me the pieces later? At the moment, just inform the sales person to reserve them for you?' Saloma replied smoothly.

'We knew you'll understand! See, I told you,' Su-Ann said, nudging Janice in the ribs. 'You're always too shy to ask!'

'By the way, where's that handsome husband of yours?' Su-Ann asked, craning her neck as she looked around the crowd. That makes two of us, Saloma thought with annoyance.

'He's somewhere,' Saloma lied with a smile. 'Let's chat later,' Saloma said as she moved to greet another guest, feeling her jaw ache from the constant smiling.

'Saloma, may I steal you for a moment?'

Saloma looked down and saw Deej smiling at her.

'Of course, Deej. Please excuse me,' Saloma addressed the elderly woman next to her, who was dressed in vintage couture from top to bottom.

'Is everything all right?' Saloma whispered to Deej.

'Yes, everything is fine,' Deej whispered back. 'Can you and Noah meet me at the hotel lobby? There's a spot that provides an ideal photo op.'

'He isn't here yet. He told me that there's an urgent meeting he had to attend,' Saloma said truthfully. 'I'm sure it dragged on, as meetings often do,' Saloma said as she waved at a guest.

'A meeting?' Deej said with a frown. 'Today?'

'Uh-huh,' Saloma replied with mild irritation. 'It's something he couldn't get out of. Anyway, it makes more sense to take a photo of me and Cass instead. It was Cass who started this atelier.'

'Yes, but we've covered that already,' Deej insisted. 'Now we need a personal story, a human angle, that'll interest the readers more. It's perfect for Valentine's Day, which you know, is just round the corner.'

'I don't want to talk about my private life, Deej. I think there's already enough coverage from when we opened the centres,' Saloma said, her voice cold.

'Well, that was before. We need a fresher, more current take of your life now,' Deej said, undeterred.

'He's not here, Deej, I guess you just have to come up with another angle. I'm sure you'd have no problem with that,' Saloma said as she accepted a glass of water from a waiter and walked away. Where was Noah, she thought with a rising sense of panic. He hadn't replied to any of her text messages and it was getting difficult to explain his absence. She spied Chris from a distance and made her way with a sigh of relief. Chris should know. She would have attended the meeting with him.

'Chris, thanks for coming! I know you had a busy morning,' Saloma said as she bent down to hug her.

'Sal, you're looking fabulous and what a turnout,' Chris exclaimed as she returned the hug. 'A busy morning?' Chris asked as she pulled away.

'Yes, I understand you had an important meeting this morning?' Saloma asked, her mouth turning dry.

'It's a Saturday, Sal. I don't work on Saturdays. Did I miss something?' Chris asked, whipping out her phone and scrolling through her emails in alarm.

'Chris, I'm sorry,' Saloma said, putting a hand on her arm. 'I must have been mistaken. Noah told me that he had a meeting to attend. I just assumed you would be there too,' Saloma said, feeling sweat trickling down her back.

'Oh, okay. But I don't think it's got to do with the centres,' Chris said as she pocketed her phone and took a glass of champagne from a waiter. 'Champagne in the day, this *is* a treat,' she said as she sipped the bubbly water with a sigh. 'Congratulations, Sal, this launch is indeed fantastic, I must get the name of the event organizer,' she said, looking around her with pleasure.

'What do you mean, Chris, when you said the meeting wouldn't be about the centres?' Saloma asked, feeling sick to her stomach.

'Well, just that. Everything is running like clockwork. That's why Noah said he'll take a few days off next week. Perhaps he's planning a surprise trip with you?' Chris asked with a wink.

'Well, it'll certainly be a surprise as I don't know anything about it!' Saloma shot back. She dug her nails into her palms and forced her lips into a smile. 'Anyway, thanks for coming Chris. Enjoy the party,' Saloma said, touching Chris lightly on the arm. Walking to a quiet corner, she reached for her handphone. Mavis, she must call Mavis.

'Mavis, do you know where Noah is?' Saloma asked without preamble, relieved when Mavis picked up her call on the first ring.

'Yes, I do.'

'And?' Saloma asked with impatience.

'He's at a hotel, not far from you actually,' Mavis said, her voice quiet.

'Hotel?' Saloma wavered. 'With her? Are you sure? He's at a meeting. He told me so early this morning.'

'There was no meeting, Saloma. He met her for brunch at a hotel, and they proceeded to one of the rooms thereafter.'

'That doesn't make sense. Noah doesn't lie. He's many things but a liar is not one of them!' Saloma took a deep breath and waited. 'Mavis?'

'I'm still here.'

'But you said the relationship is still in the early stages,' Saloma said, trying and failing to hide her accusatory tone. 'Mavis?'

'I'm listening.'

'But why the hell aren't you saying anything?' Saloma shrieked, lowering her voice immediately when one of the guests turned to look at her. Taking a deep breath, she strode to an empty bench, away from the crowd.

'Mavis, I don't understand this development,' Saloma continued, wiping her damp hands on the leg of her trousers. 'He said he'll be at my launch, albeit after his meeting. He said so, twice! I've been planning this for months, for goodness' sake! It's not like him to do this to me. You must have made a mistake,' Saloma insisted, feeling her voice tremble.

'I heard you, Saloma, but the way things are, I doubt he'll be at your launch. He's been with her the whole time.'

'He chose today of all days? It's my launch, for goodness' sake! It's *my* day!' Saloma screeched, hearing the childish indignation in her voice. 'Yet everyone is looking for him. And I'm running out of excuses,' Saloma said, clearing her throat. 'I still don't understand, Mavis. He was happy for me, I mean . . . he seemed happy,' Saloma said, now unsure. 'Mavis?'

'I'm still here, Saloma. How do you like me to proceed?'

'End it Mavis! Do you hear me?'

'Yes, absolutely. Of course, I'll set it in motion.'

'Yes, do that! That's why I pay you and *her* a shitload of money!' Saloma said as she ended the call, her chest heaving. She walked to an empty washroom and chose a stall at the far end. Slamming the toilet seat down, she sat down with a bump, staring at the door. Her shoulders started to heave, and she began to laugh. She laughed hard and loud, till it hurt.

Chapter 31

Saloma reached out and touched the empty pillow next to hers. It felt cold to her touch. She turned on her back and stared at the ceiling, the ticking of her bedside clock, the only sound in the bedroom. Moving restlessly, under the sheets, she plumped up her pillow and willed herself to sleep. She knew Cass had noticed her weight loss and the dark circles under her eyes. It would be a matter of time before she dug the truth out of her. The truth? What was the truth? Did it even matter now? Saloma let out a sigh and glanced at her clock, the green hands glowing in the dark. It was barely five in the morning. Was Noah with her? Of course he was, she thought, feeling the familiar tightness on her chest. His detailed whereabouts were sent to her every day, but she hadn't seen him in a week. Other than the text message of, 'I'll be away for a couple of days,' which she received after her launch, she hadn't heard from him. She had responded with a deluge of messages on her part, relieved he had replied yet angry at his disappearance, but he remained silent. He'll come around, she thought, turning on her side and staring at the empty space next to hers. It's just a matter of time before he comes around to realize how much he needed her.

She gave up the pretence of sleeping and threw back the covers. Barefooted, she made her way to the kitchen and drank a glass of water straight from the kitchen tap. Her eyes strayed to the colourful country magnets that covered the fridge door. They were Noah's collection. 'A quirky touch to your otherwise minimalist kitchen,' he had said, with laughter. 'It's *our* kitchen, Noah,' she had stressed but he had shrugged and walked away. She fingered the jumbo magnet he got from Spain and bit her lip. Has she gone too far in doing things her way? She made her way to the living room in the dark and curled herself up in the white three-seater sofa and closed her eyes. She fell into an uneasy sleep and woke up to a crick in her neck and sunlight streaming through the crack in the floor length curtains. She lay on her back and stretched out her cramped limbs, massaging her neck until she heard a key turn in the lock. She froze for a second before scrambling off the sofa and ran to the front door. Saloma held her breath as the door squeaked open and Noah entered the front lobby, dressed casually in jeans and a black shirt.

'Noah,' she gasped, taking a few steps towards him but stopping midway, unsure.

'You're home,' he said, walking into the hallway with his sneakers on.

'Of course. Where else would I be? Noah, take off your shoes,' she said with a nervous laugh.

'I won't be long,' he said, striding to their storage cupboard and rolling out two empty suitcases.

'Noah, what are you doing? Where are you going?' Saloma whispered.

Noah turned and looked at her, his eyes giving nothing away. Saloma clutched the back of a chair and steadied herself.

He walked to their bedroom, rolling and carrying the suitcases both at the same time.

Saloma followed closely, feeling her stomach churning. She stopped at the doorway, as he flung the suitcases on the bed and opened them wide. He grabbed an armful of his clothes and filled up the suitcases, his movements quick and decisive.

Saloma walked into the room and sat at a corner of the bed, feeling sick. 'Noah, talk to me, what's going on.'

He glanced at her briefly but continued to pack, leaving his shirts, still in their hangers, in a small pile on the bed.

'You'll know soon enough, won't you,' he said, lifting an eyebrow.

'I still don't understand,' Saloma said, digging her nails into her palms, her head swimming.

'Oh you, do, Saloma, you do,' Noah said, pulling out the drawers and emptying them into the cases.

Saloma flinched when she heard her full name. 'Stop it, Noah, stop packing,' she said, walking towards him and reaching out to touch his arm. The muscles tensed under her touch, and Saloma let her hand fall to her side.

'Where are you going?' Saloma repeated for the second time.

'Out. Isn't it obvious?' Noah said, as he closed the suitcases and placed his shirts in a garment bag. 'I'll collect the rest of my things another day, and I'll leave the key on the dining table.'

Saloma felt her knees tremble and sat at the edge of the bed.

'Keys? You mean the keys to this apartment, our . . . our home?' she stammered.

'Home? This is home? Really,' Noah asked, his voice disbelieving.

Saloma looked down and gripped her hands tight, almost in a prayer.

'Talk to me, sayang, please.'

'It's over,' he said, walking out of the bedroom with the luggage in tow.

Saloma willed her legs to stand and trailed behind him, wondering if she was still asleep. 'Noah, please. Explain this to me.' She watched him as he placed the suitcases next to the front door and draped his garment bag over them. A guttural sound escaped her lips, when he reached to open the front door. 'Noah, please. Please don't leave,' she said, wiping her tears with the back of her hand.

He turned around and walked back towards Saloma.

'You really have no idea what's going on, huh?' he asked, looking at her with narrowed eyes.

Saloma returned his stare and shook her head.

'I know what you did. I knew it for quite a while now,' Noah said, hands in his pockets.

Saloma dropped into a nearest chair and moved her lips but as much as she tried, no sound came from them. 'What do you mean?' she managed at last, biting her lips till she felt blood in her mouth.

'I don't have time for games, Saloma,' Noah said as he reached for the door handle.

'Wait! All right,' Saloma said, taking a deep breath. 'What is that you know and how?'

Noah shrugged. 'Everything. Yes, everything,' he repeated to the incredulous look in her eyes. 'I knew it was you who informed Chris about Sam. You made it your business to expel her in the cruellest way. I wasn't sure at first, but with Sam's help, I discovered a private investigator was hired and it was a matter of time, a long time I must add, that I found out it was you.'

'But she was out to get you! Don't you see, I did it for us!' Saloma cried out.

'And you didn't think I could decide that for myself?'

'She was pursuing you! You have no idea how desperate a woman can be!'

'I think I do. I most certainly do,' Noah said, his voice soft.

Saloma stood up and walked towards him, putting her arms around his neck.

He stood still.

'You need me, I'm the only one who can fulfil you. We're meant for each other. I love you,' she whispered in his chest.

Noah removed her arms around his neck and took a step back. 'I don't think you even know what that means.'

'What? What are you saying?' Saloma asked, brushing her hair out of her eyes.

'Love? You know nothing about it. If you did, you wouldn't have stooped so low as to hire women to ensnare me.'

'You knew about that too, and you strung me along!' Saloma shouted.

Noah rocked on his heels and took his time answering. 'I had to know how far you would go.' He paused. 'You underestimated me. You didn't think that I could get the truth out of the two women you hired?'

'I did it for us! Don't you see! I want you to see that I'm the only one who loves you, who will do anything to keep us together. I don't want to confine you. Men need their space, their freedom. As long as you come home to me, nothing else matters!'

Noah stared at her, his shoulders taut and his jaw working furiously. 'Where do you get your narratives from? From your mother? Or from the dramas she watches?' he asked, his voice laced with sarcasm. 'What am I, Saloma? Some caveman who can't control his needs? And how long do you intend to do this? Throughout the course of our marriage? How many women would that be?'

Saloma recoiled as if he'd hit her.

'Not once did it occur to you that I respect the vows *I made* when we got married?' Noah continued unabated.

'Um . . . yes, of course,' Saloma stammered. 'But things changed, *you* changed and I had to do something! And don't go all puritanical on me,' Saloma shot back. 'I know you've been spending time with her, in a hotel.'

Noah rubbed his jaw and closed his eyes briefly. 'Yes, I stayed in a hotel room with Marianne but I took the couch and she took the bed. I've been faithful to you throughout our marriage, Saloma, even though you don't think fidelity is important,' Noah said, looking at her briefly. He paused. 'Well, as it turned out, Marianne and I enjoyed our talks. I may want to see her again.'

'You want to date a prostitute?' Saloma asked with a laugh.

'She isn't. Didn't you tell your private investigator you wanted someone innocent, someone real,' he said with a twist of his mouth. 'Be careful what you ask for cos as it turned out, she is. Yes, she did it for the money, but it was to pay for her mother's medical care and for her brother's education.'

'And you believed her sob story?' Saloma asked incredulously.

'There *are* honest people out there in the world. Some of them have to make difficult choices and she's one of them. *You* could have chosen to talk to me, shared with me,' Noah said, his head cocked to one side.

'Talk?' Saloma sneered. 'How could I possibly talk to or with you. Half the time, you just clam up and walk away. What else could I do but make assumptions. I'm only human.'

'That's not true. There were several occasions I suggested, even insisted to get away, to have a respite from everything but you refused.'

'Of course, I refused! How could we get away when we were in the middle of a business development or a crisis!'

'I don't give a damn about the business. It's just money. We can earn it again. What mattered to me then was you, us, our marriage.'

'Money can be earned again?' Saloma echoed in disbelief. 'Are you serious? Have you any idea how hard I worked to get where we are right now? The sacrifices I *made*. You didn't have to go through a third of the prejudices I went through. I mean, how could you. Just look at you,' Saloma spat, giving him a run down. 'You may be of mixed race, but you look practically white, the seas part for you. You're as privileged as the Chinese!'

'And how much is enough, Saloma?' Noah asked, his voice so quiet she had to move closer to hear him.

'As much as possible! So much, that colour does not matter!'

'Don't you see that regardless of how much you make, they will never see you as one of them. I don't know why you need to be them, anyway. Why does that equal success?'

'That's not true! They do see me as one of them,' Saloma insisted. 'And you can't possibly be so naïve! Success is dictated by them, they call the shots, naturally, I have to work towards being accepted by them. How is it that you don't get it? Anyway, if money doesn't matter to you, why didn't you stop the expansion of the centres!' Saloma demanded.

'Yes, I could have stopped the growth but I was stunned by the overwhelming response or interest. I don't know,' Noah stared at his shoes.

'I don't believe I'm hearing this now!' she said, indignant. 'You didn't put a stop to it and yet you turn around *now* and accuse me of . . . of what, being obsessive about money,' she screamed. 'You . . . you allowed me to handle the finances,' Saloma said, pointing at him with her forefinger, 'and now you have the temerity to say that I'm . . . I'm money faced!' she spat out.

'I don't think I'd have been able to stop you,' Noah said. He rubbed his nape and said softly, 'I'll buy out your shares at the Skills Lab. You can have this apartment and of course, your jewellery business,' he said, looking at her in the eye.

'What are you saying? Am I not making sense? I've just explained it to you,' Saloma said, her chest heaving. 'I'm not the same colour as you, Noah,' she said, her voice wavered. 'You'll never understand what I went through or . . . or the hunger to succeed, to fight for what I want, what I deserve. I had to work so much harder, being a woman and a minority. Why am I being punished?' she cried out. 'Look, I forgive you for not understanding my challenges, but you have to understand that I did it for both of us.' Saloma took a deep breath and threw caution to the wind. 'And where will you be without me, Noah?

It was me who made your business successful, made it what it is today. You're just a teacher.'

'And your solution for this is to hire women for me?' Noah asked in disbelief.

'Yes, cos I have to do everything, right, Noah?' Saloma asked.

'So, I've done nothing? It was my style of teaching, my curriculum that shaped the centres. I gave purpose to the business.'

Saloma wrapped her arms around her body, feeling cold.

'It's over. I'm divorcing you and with all the evidence I have, I suggest you accept it,' Noah said, picking up his garment bag.

'But I don't want a divorce. We've built all of this together. How am I going to explain to the press, to our clients, and friends!' Saloma screamed. 'I don't want a divorce!' Saloma reached out and touched his face. 'I did it for us!'

'No.' Noah pulled open the door but Saloma ran past him and slammed it shut with her body.

'I'll make changes, Noah. You can have a relationship with Marianne, I don't care. Just stay with me,' Saloma said with a sob.

'I'm done being your prop. You use the people around you, Saloma.'

Saloma gasped for breath, her eyes huge in her pale face.

'I feel sorry for you. You're a sum of other people's beliefs. You've allowed them to suck the humanity out of you, leaving you nothing but a mock person. You're just,' Noah let his eyes wander over her, taking his time, 'a shell.' He pushed her away and stepped out of the door.

Chapter 32

Saloma squinted at the early afternoon sunshine, feeling sweat pricking her back under her light cotton blouse. The taxi stand was empty, and she sat at the edge of the orange plastic seat, feeling the heat through her trousers. She reached for her sunglasses, grateful for the dark lenses, and like the rest of the nation, wished for rain, lots of rain.

'Sal, is that you? Why aren't you driving?'

Saloma looked up and found herself staring at Deej, dressed in jeans and a t-shirt.

'Not working today?' Saloma asked instead.

'Yes,' Deej, said with a laugh, sitting next to Saloma and fanning herself with a brochure. 'Just for today. I had some chores to do, and just stopped by the office to drop off some papers for Cass. So, you're not driving today?' she repeated.

Saloma shrugged. 'I don't have a car.'

Deej stopped and stared at her, open mouthed. 'You sold it? Your fancy sports car?'

'Yup.'

'So, what are you getting now?'

'I'm not too sure, I haven't decided.'

Deej stuffed the brochure in her bag and cleared her throat. 'I heard about you and Noah. I've been meaning to tell you how sorry I am and that . . . well, if I can help in any way, do let me know,' she said, her eyes open and honest.

'Thanks, Deej, I appreciate it,' Saloma said, knowing that Deej was sincere.

'Um . . . I know you've been staying with Cass for the last three months and thinking of putting up your apartment for sale. I've got a good real estate agent if you need one.'

'That would be helpful. Thanks, Deej.'

They sat without talking for a few minutes, facing each other. Deej shifted in her seat and fidgeted with the straps of her bag.

'By the way, I've been meaning to ask you, were you named after *Saloma*? That Saloma?' Deej asked.

'Yes, the famous Malay actress called Saloma. From the 60's, I think. My parents were fans of Saloma and her husband P. Ramlee.'

'Aha. Now I understand the tune you're always humming,' Deej said under her breath.

'I don't understand,' Saloma said, genuinely puzzled.

'It's just something I noticed, that tune you're always humming,' Deej explained.

'Oh that,' Saloma said, feeling a blush spreading her face. 'I picked it up from my late father. I think it's from an old movie.'

'Yes, it is. It's called *Madu Tiga*. My mother happened to watch this ridiculous movie when I visited her last weekend. Do you know the story?'

Saloma shook her head, perplexed.

'It's about a husband who married two other women without his wife's knowledge but secretly, got the blessings of his father-in-law. That was funny but what irked me was that in the end, the three women lived happily ever after with him, the philanderer.' Deej shook her head. 'Strange, how the Malay community viewed men back then. No way this could happen in the twenty-first century, especially here, in Singapore. Can you imagine, an educated, hardworking woman sharing her husband with not one, but two women and to add insult to injury, have them live with you under one roof! Ridiculous. Anyway, it was a catchy tune,' Deej rambled on.

'Oh,' Saloma said, at loss for words. 'My cab is here. Enjoy your afternoon,' Saloma said as she walked towards the waiting car and opened the passenger door.

'You too!' Deej hollered, waving at her.

Saloma settled herself in the seat and turned the air conditioning to the maximum.

'Wah, you're so pretty! From Spain, Italy?' the taxi driver uttered with no shame.

Saloma glanced at the rear-view mirror and caught the eye of the driver. 'I'm from Singapore. And I'm Malay.'

Acknowledgements

I would like to thank the following people who have made this novel a reality:

I have to start with my husband, Ramesh, who has been in this writing journey of mine for more than twenty years. He has read every single draft—a barometer for what is good, awful and everything in between. He's my sounding board, my first reader, and editor all rolled into one.

To my creative and artistic daughter Sarah, who made it her mission to remind me of the importance of symbolism and good dialogue. With her invaluable help, I strived to create complex nuances in the story and to give my characters a more emotional dimension in their conversations.

To my sister Afidah, who shared with me the background on the setting up of tuition centres and for her support and encouragement.

To the team of Penguin Random House Southeast Asia, in particular, my publisher, Nora Abu Bakar, who gave me this unbelievable opportunity, and to my editor, Thatchaayanie Renganathan, for her discerning editing eye in making my novel a tighter, better read.

Last but not least, to Ashidah, who saw a writer in me long before I knew it.